# OLD SOLDIERS NEVER DIE

*A Selection of Recent Titles by Margaret Mayhew*

BLUEBIRDS
THE CREW

# OLD SOLDIERS NEVER DIE

## Margaret Mayhew

This first world edition published in Great Britain 1999 by
SEVERN HOUSE PUBLISHERS LTD of
9–15 High Street, Sutton, Surrey SM1 1DF.
This title first published in the U.S.A. 1999 by
SEVERN HOUSE PUBLISHERS INC of
595 Madison Avenue, New York, N.Y. 10022.

Copyright © 1999 by Margaret Mayhew.

All rights reserved.
The moral right of the author has been asserted.

*To Gilly*

British Library Cataloguing in Publication Data

Mayhew, Margaret
    Old soldiers never die
    1. Detective and mystery stories
    I. Title
    823.9'14 [F]

    ISBN 0-7278-5441-0

All situations in this publication are fictitious and
any resemblance to living persons is purely coincidental.

Typeset by Hewer Text Ltd
Edinburgh, Scotland.
Printed and bound in Great Britain by
MPG Books Ltd, Bodmin, Cornwall.

# One

The Colonel moved into his cottage at Frog End on a fine day in spring. It was called Pond Cottage, though, as far as he could see, there was no sign of any such thing. The local estate agent – an eager young man in a creased blazer and scuffed suede shoes – had described it as having potential when he first showed him round. Potential, the Colonel had learned later, meant that although the place was dilapidated, it wasn't actually falling down and, with a lot of work and considerable expense, it could probably be made to look quite passable.

The survey had been a disaster and he had bought the cottage against all sanity and reason. A bungalow would have been far more sensible – preferably brand new, like the one he had also viewed in another part of the village which was, appropriately, called Journey's End. There would have been efficient central heating, modern wiring and plumbing, a proper damp course, easy-to-clean wood and vinyl floors, plastic guttering and drainpipes, and rot-proof metal-framed windows. And, outside, there would have been a manageable square plot for a garden – mainly lawn and cement paving, with two small flowerbeds.

Instead, he had landed himself with a two-hundred-year-old thatched dwelling that had death-watch beatle, rising damp, a falling roof, rot and decay throughout and half an acre or more of impenetrable jungle. There was no proper heating of any kind – unless one counted the ancient range in the kitchen and the ugly little tiled fireplace in the sitting-room – and the wiring was a dangerous disgrace. Wood for the range and coal for the fire had been kept in the claw-foot bath in the scullery and the lavatory was in an outhouse, surrounded by a hostile barrier of nettles. The previous occupant, a tenant, had apparently been an old man who had lived to more than ninety, long after his wife had died, and obviously in some squalor. When the old man's turn had finally come, the owner, a local farmer, had scarcely waited until he had been carried out, feet first, before putting the place on the market for the highest price that he had had the nerve to ask.

Why, then, had the Colonel bought it instead of the bungalow? It was much cheaper, but that had nothing to do with it. It was because Laura had once seen it and liked it. Years ago when they had been touring the West Country back on leave one summer, they had driven at random through the Dorset lanes, discovering countryside and hamlets still almost untouched by the twentieth century. Real Thomas Hardy country, Laura had called it, gazing delightedly out of the car window. She used to read all Hardy's books, and the Brontes, and George Eliot and Mrs Gaskell . . . all that sort of thing. Military history was more his line, and biographies. And a good thriller or detective story when he was feeling more tired than usual and wanted to relax.

They'd come across Frog End quite by chance. The narrow lane they had taken seemed to lead to nowhere in particular. There had been a pretty little water splash across the road with some ducks paddling about and he'd had to go very slowly while they got out of the way, quacking indignantly. Then he'd driven round a corner and the village had suddenly appeared before them, serene and beautiful in the sunlight . . .

at peace under an English heaven. The Colonel was weak on Hardy but he knew his Brooke. The village green had a pond, with more ducks, and a cluster of old stone cottages about it. There was a Norman church and, inevitably, a pub. The Dog and Duck had been a very simple place then, just a couple of rooms with flagstone floors, offering good draft beer and plain sandwiches – cheese and pickle, ham and mustard, and packets of plain Smith's crisps with salt in a blue paper twist. No-frills fare. They'd sat outside on a wooden bench, and noticed the cottage on the far side of the green. A climbing rose had been in full bloom over the porch, the pink flowers smothering the stone walls. In the sunshine, and from a safe distance, it had looked enchanting. Laura had remarked on it and said that it was just the sort of place she dreamed they'd live in one day when he retired from the army and they could settle down in England. He'd agreed with her. One day, they'd promised themselves, drinking the beer and eating the sandwiches and looking across the green. One day.

 He had forgotten all about the cottage until many years later, after Laura had died. He had gone to stay with old friends in Dorset and on the way had driven round the countryside, trying to retrace some of the places he had visited with Laura. Places they had been together and experiences they had known and shared, brought her back to him, if only for a while. He had managed to find Frog End again, more by luck than anything, as he had forgotten its name. He had stopped for lunch at the Dog and Duck which had gone and tarted itself up since their visit. The nice old flagstones had vanished beneath red and green geometrically patterned carpeting and there was the cheap glint of modern copper and brass and the synthetic shine of plastic. A new extension had been built onto the back, complete with mock beams, where they served full meals now: steak and kidney pie, chili con carne, lasagne, chicken in a basket, scampi and chips, prawn salad – not bad if you didn't mind the prices. But the beer wasn't a patch on the draft they'd served that day he'd been there with Laura.

It had been late autumn and too cold to sit outside, but afterwards he had driven round the green. In pouring rain and under leaden skies the village had not looked quite so idyllic, but he had noticed that Laura's dream cottage was up for sale. At first he had not recognised it without its pink roses, and, close to, it had proved more of a nightmare. Either distance had lent enchantment, or it had gone downhill badly in the intervening years. Come to that, the whole village had changed since he had last seen it. Apart from the spoiling of the pub there was a raw outcrop of new houses at the far end of the green – one of them the bungalow, Journey's End.

He had never intended to go and bury himself in the depths of Dorset. After Laura had died he had stayed on in the small London flat. It was fairly close to Alison – not that he wanted to interfere in his daughter's life – and it was also where the work was. Or where he hoped it would be. In the same year as Laura's death he had reached the grand old age of fifty-five when the army retired you whether you wanted it or not. His services had been summarily dispensed with and he had been put out to grass. Unthinkable, of course. Far too young to do nothing but, unfortunately, too old to start a new career, as he had soon discovered. He had lost count of the number of jobs he had applied for: thirty-seven years in the army, apparently, counted for nothing in the outside world. Finally, he had landed the post of bursar in a private day school in Hampstead. The school had progressive ideas on education and even more progressive ones on discipline that were not only baffling to him but a positive affront. The pupils, boys and girls, were the teenage children of the very rich, many of them foreign, most of them spoilt rotten and nearly all of them grossly neglected by their parents. He stuck it out for five long years before resigning when he could stand the laxity no longer. After that, he had spent nearly a year job hunting again before being taken on by a double-glazing company to cold call potential customers. He had got the job, he later discovered, because they thought his voice would inspire confidence. He had lasted for six months before they decided it didn't and replaced him with a fast-talking Artful Dodger thirty years his junior. After that he had found temporary work on trade stands at exhibitions, as a crowd extra in several film productions and, via that, as the smartly dressed older man in the background for some glossy advertisements for women's clothing. When, at the age of sixty-five, he had answered a promising, but vaguely worded advertisement and found it was to sell brushes and cleaning materials door-to-door, he had decided to call it a day.

The question was, where to spend his enforced retirement? London, he had discovered, was not only an expensive place to live on an army pension, but extremely lonely. He and Laura had spent almost all their married life abroad, stationed in different parts of the world, and he knew very few people in the city. Alison had her own life to lead, busy in her PR job, and he had no right to depend on her for company. Marcus, his son, kept urging him to go and live near him and his family in the Midlands but he knew that would be fatal. His daughter-in-law, Susan, would be round with meals on wheels in a flash, driving him mad.

The visit to his old friends in Dorset had come at the lowest point in his life. Over lunch he had told them about seeing the cottage for sale and they had been enthusiastic. The country would be far better for him, they had said with great confidence. He'd meet people far more easily living in a village, and it would provide him with all sorts of activities to take up his time: serving on the local parish council, perhaps; becoming a church warden; acting as secretary or treasurer to a club; helping with the parish magazine; taking up bell ringing; lecturing on his army travels to Women's Institutes, and so on. There was quite a long list of options. In the end he had convinced himself that they were right, and, for all its faults, Pond Cottage, had seemed a friendly sort of place. It had a good atmosphere and, fortunately, the young estate agent had been proved right about the 'potential'.

He watched the removal men unloading his worldly goods. Two containers of stuff that had been in Harrods Depository since heaven knew when, and another of everything that he and Laura had carted round the world to every posting – pictures, lamps, bedding, books, ornaments, or what was still left unbroken on this final trip. He scarcely recognised some of the items emerging from the Harrods lot – things he had long forgotten about and some he could swear he and Laura had never owned. What was that tapestry wing-back chair they were carrying past? And that spindly little piecrust table? And the large mahogany sideboard perched drunkenly on the lowered tailgate, awaiting its turn? They must have belonged to Laura's mother and been passed on at her death. He would last have seen them in that gloomy flat in Phillimore Gardens, though he had no recollection of them at all.

The foreman of the removal team was brandishing the piecrust table by its one leg from the doorway. "Where d'you want this one, guv?"

He went inside and directed operations. Since his first visit with the eager young estate agent, the cottage had undergone a sea change. The roof had been re-thatched and builders had been in for weeks, tearing down false ceilings to expose old beams, replacing rotten timbers, re-plastering walls, opening

## Old Soldiers Never Die

up the old inglenook that had turned out to lie behind the tiled fireplace, re-plumbing and re-wiring, installing oil-fired central heating, turning a bedroom into a bathroom, re-fitting the kitchen . . . on and on it had gone through the dark winter months. Then the painters had arrived with large pots of magnolia emulsion and matt white vinyl paint, followed by the carpet layer and a woman from the shop in Dorchester that he had found to do the curtains – chintz for the bedrooms, plain for the rest. He had chosen from a mountain of swatches at random and without any real interest, while she had hovered irritatingly at his shoulder. It was unbearable to think how much Laura would have enjoyed choosing everything, and how well she would have done it. However grim and drear their married quarters had been – and some had been extremely so – she had always managed to transform them. The ornaments and pictures, lamps, cushions and books had been unpacked and put round, the vases filled with flowers and, in a twinkling of an eye, the place was home. It was a gift, he had decided, seeing what other army wives had made of similar places. Or failed to make. It had nothing to do with expensive fabrics and furnishings, still less with trendy interior designers. It was a knack that some women had, and some did not.

The sideboard was unwilling to make its entrance into the tiny dining room and he took refuge in the kitchen while the men were struggling and cursing over it. Would Laura have approved of what he had done in here? The cabinets were pine, chosen from a catalogue because he thought they looked pleasant, and the sink was made of white porcelain because he could vaguely remember Laura once saying that was the best kind to have. There was no gas in the village and so the cooker was electric. It stood there, sandwiched neatly between two units, gleamingly white and new, and utterly alien to him. In the London flat he had cooked on an old gas stove, though 'cooked' was the wrong word. Heated up would describe it better: stuff out of tins, ready-made dishes in foil trays and frozen vegetables. He had bought a small microwave oven, too, because the woman in the electricity shop had kept telling him how useful it would be for baking potatoes and defrosting things. He'd given in more out of politeness than any interest in what you could do with it. In spite of the builders' head-shaking bewilderment, he had kept the iron range. Somehow he liked the look of the old thing, and he had an idea that Laura would have agreed. It had been cleaned out, de-rusted and black-leaded and stood revealed in all its former glory. He had no practical use for it but, it was far more friendly-looking than the modern cooker and he was glad he'd spared it from the dump.

He looked out into the hall. The sideboard had evidently surrendered and gone quietly but there were now more muffled curses coming from the direction of the narrow oak staircase. The foreman descended, wiping his forehead. "That bed won't go up that stairway, guv. Not an 'ope."

The bed was the one that he and Laura had bought at the start of their married life and Alison and Marcus had both been conceived in it. It had never occured to him that there would be a problem in getting it up the stairs.

"It's the bend, guv," the foreman explained with happy pessimism. "Can't get 'er round it, see. Can't be done."

"Would you give it another try, please?"

An expressive shrug. "If you want. But like I say, there's not an 'ope."

They grunted and struggled some more, to-ing and fro-ing at the turn halfway up the stairs, and then suddenly up she went and he could hear them bumping about in the bedroom overhead.

## Old Soldiers Never Die

"Bloomin' miracle that," the foreman told him when he came down. He seemed aggrieved to have succeeded.

It was early evening before they had finished and gone off with a handsome tip. The big removal lorry ground noisily away and, left alone, the Colonel stood in the silence of the cottage. Even after ten years, he still could not get used to that silence. Until Laura had died, and for as long as he could remember, there had been other people around – his parents, his brother, his schoolfriends, his fellow officers, and then Laura and the children. There had always been someone there, something going on, never this terrible silence, so total and so oppressive that it was almost audible. Searching for something to break it, he fiddled with the weights and pendulum inside the grandfather clock that the men had deposited in a corner of the sitting-room and, after all its silent years in store, the reassuring tick-tock began again. He hunted for a glass, poured a stiff shot from the bottle of Chivas Regal that he had had the presence of mind to get, and sat down in the wing-back tapestry chair, which turned out to be rather comfortable. As he did so, the clock struck six with quick, silvery chimes. Odd to hear it again. It had belonged to his parents and he knew the sound from childhood. Listening to it took him straight back to the rambling Victorian house in North London where it had stood in the hall, ticking and chiming away as he grew up. He used to play there with his toy cars, scooting them very fast across the tiled floor. If he looked hard, he would probably find the small dents and marks at the base where they had smacked into it. The clock had ticked on steadily through the years, always there in the hall as he came and went from prep school, then public school, then Sandhurst, evolving gradually from the small boy crawling around at its foot to the six-foot-two young soldier who could look it straight in the face.

## Margaret Mayhew

The Colonel drank his whisky reflectively. The best way forward now, he supposed, with irony, was to look backward. To settle for living in the past, since the present was so unappealing. Let alone the future.

> To-morrow, and to-morrow, and to-morrow,
> Creeps in this petty pace from day to day,
> To the last syllable of recorded time

The Colonel knew his Shakespeare as well as his Brooke, and his Masefield and his Wordsworth and his Coleridge and his Keats and his Tennyson . . . They were all among the boxes of books waiting to be unpacked and put away on the new shelves along one wall of the sitting-room. And all around him were other boxes, also waiting, full of ornaments and pictures and lamps – none of which he had the energy to deal with. He didn't much care where anything went, or what the cottage looked like since Laura was not there to share it with him. He drank some more whisky and shut his eyes for a moment, leaning his head against the back of the chair. When he opened them again he saw a cat sitting watching him in the sitting-room doorway. It gave him a bit of a shock, the way it had just appeared without a sound. Damn it, he must have left the front door open. It was a battle-scarred old thing with a torn ear and a motley black and tan coat. He'd have to throw it out.

"Hello, Puss. Where've you sprung from?"

The cat blinked at him slowly and then walked into the room and all round it, sniffing at the cardboard boxes, tail twitching.

"Sorry, you can't stay here. Off you go!"

He clapped his hands firmly. The cat ignored him and jumped up onto the sofa; it clawed at the cushioning once or

## Old Soldiers Never Die

twice and then settled down comfortably, paws folded under its chin. In addition to the tick-tock from the clock there was now the sound of loud purring. And then another sound, much less soothing.

"Hellooo! Anyone at home?"

He swore under his breath. Why the hell hadn't he shut the door? First some stray cat, then some bloody woman yelling at him. Perhaps if he kept very quiet she'd go away.

"*Colonel?* Are you there?"

He sighed and rose to his feet. That was the voice of an elderly English female baying after a strong scent and in his experience it was highly unlikely that she would be put off easily. Indeed, the voice had moved nearer and, as he started towards the sitting-room doorway, its owner appeared.

She was dressed, not in the conventional country tweeds and brogues that he had expected, but in a purple tracksuit and white running shoes. And she was no frail little old faded thing, but a big woman who filled the doorway with her bulk. Her thick grey hair was cut very short, like a thatch, above a round, healthily pink face, and her blue eyes were clear and alert. She stuck out a large hand.

"Naomi Grimshaw, Colonel. Pleased to meet you. I'm your neighbour." She jerked the thatch to her right. "Pear Tree Cottage, next door."

He took the hand; it felt as rough as sandpaper. A gardener's hand, he thought, remembering his glimpse of the next-door garden from an upstairs window, over the stone wall that divided them. He had admired the white blossom (presumably pear tree), some drifts of yellow in the far corner, the burgeoning shrubs, the pale pink cascade of something growing over a wall. He knew nothing about plants but he recognised the work of a natural-born gardener when he saw it.

"Mrs? Miss?" It was hard to tell and she wore no rings. He

noticed, though, that she sported an outsize man's watch on her left wrist which looked as though it was meant for serious deep-sea diving.

"Mrs. Widowed like yourself. But call me Naomi. At our age we can't afford to waste any time."

He smiled. In spite of the trendy clothing she was, indeed, probably about the same age as himself and the remark was open to misinterpretation. But it had been offered without a trace of archness. The village grapevine was already evidently well-informed on his marital status.

"Hugh." He released her hand.

She was peering past him at the sitting-room. "Looks rather better than it did, I must say. A real transformation. I see Thursday has come back."

"Thursday?"

She nodded at the sofa. "The tom. He belonged to old Ben. Went off when he died. He must have seen you moving in and decided he liked the look of you. Don't worry, he's been neutered. I made Ben get him done to stop him fighting."

"Why Thursday?"

"He was a stray. Turned up on a Thursday so Ben called him that. Couldn't think of anything else. Come to think of it, it's Thursday today, too. Maybe he knows the days of the week. Clever things cats, though I prefer dogs, myself. Got two Jack Russells." Her eye fell on his half-empty tumbler on the piecrust table beside the chair. "Ah . . ."

"Will you join me?" he said quickly. "I'm afraid I've only got whisky."

"Love to." She plonked herself down on the sofa beside the cat, knees apart, feet firmly planted on the new green carpet; the training shoes made them look huge, he had never fathomed why women chose to wear such ugly, unflattering things in ordinary daily life.

*Old Soldiers Never Die*

"Water?"

"Just a dash. Don't drown it."

"I'm sorry there's no ice at the moment."

"Don't care. Can't understand what the Americans see in the stuff. They put so much in there's no room left for a decent drink."

He went into the kitchen in search of another glass and poured a measure as stiff as his own that he guessed would meet with her approval.

She took it from him, looked at it and sniffed. "Chivas? Can't afford that often myself. What a treat!" She raised the glass happily in his direction. "Welcome to Frog End, Hugh. I'm going to enjoy having you as a neighbour."

# Two

"Pour me a gin and tonic, please, Ruth. A large one. The Vicar's been here for more than an hour and I need it."

Lady Swynford collapsed dramatically onto the sofa and her black poodle jumped up beside her. Her daughter, Ruth, who had just entered the drawing-room, altered course for the drinks tray and held up a glass in one hand and a bottle of Gordon's in the other.

"How strong?"

"Strong enough to revive me from being practically bored to death. He really is a tedious little man. Always going on and on about the most tiresome parish affairs. I am not remotely interested in the Mothers' Union meetings, or the bible readings on Thursday evenings in his hideous bungalow, *or* the senior citizens' teas at the village hall . . . mostly especially *not* those. I can't imagine why he thinks I would be."

"I expect he feels he ought to tell you everything that's going on." Ruth carried the drink over to the sofa. "Is that all right?"

Her mother took the glass and sipped. "Rather too little gin, but it will do. Of course, he really wanted to talk about holding the church fête here again in July. That's what he came for. The whole village always seems to think they have the automatic right to do so."

"Well, it's been held at the Manor for years."

"And for years it's been a complete nuisance. All the villagers trampling over the garden and stakes being hammered into the lawn – it takes months for it all to recover. And if it's wet they want to bring their wretched stalls into the house. With so much riff-raff living in the village now, it means putting away absolutely anything of any value or it will certainly be stolen, like that silver the year before last. I told the Vicar I didn't think I could face it again. Not after I've been ill. He'll have to find somewhere else."

"I'm not sure there *is* anywhere else in the village, not with a large enough garden, not since they built on the Hall's."

"Thanks to those idiot sisters selling the whole lot off." Lady Swynford stroked the poodle lying on the sofa beside her.

"They probably needed the money."

"They can't have been *that* poor, surely. I heard they asked a ridiculously low sum and then of course that dreadful developer snapped it up. It's completely ruined the village. Strangers are moving in in droves. The Vicar told me that Pond Cottage has just been bought by some retired army colonel. A widower. Thanks heavens it's still too far for London commuters."

Ruth Swynford had poured herself a drink and sat down. The contrast between mother and daughter could not have been greater: Lady Swynford, still beautiful in her sixties, expensively elegant, carefully coiffured, manicured and made-up; Ruth, in her mid-thirties, scruffy in old corduroy trousers and a man's check shirt, her face bare of make-up and her hair cut by herself with the kitchen scissors. Her fingernails were rimmed with grime from potting-on in the greenhouse. She looked at them absently.

*Old Soldiers Never Die*

"If they improve the train service it may not be too far for much longer."

Lady Swynford shuddered. "Bank clerks and shop assistants!" She fed a chocolate to the poodle from a box on the table.

"Hardly, with those fares. More likely company directors who can afford them."

"You'd never want to do that, of course."

It was half a question, half a statement. "No, I'd never want to do that, Mama, even if I could afford it. I've finished with London. You don't need to worry."

"Well, it's not as though you were anything terribly important, is it?" She gave the poodle another chocolate. "Just a secretary. It wasn't a real *career*."

"No . . . it wasn't. He'll get fat if you keep giving him those."

"He adores them, though, don't you, Shoo-Shoo? Of course, I expect I could have managed perfectly well on my own."

"Dr Harvey didn't think so, and he should know. You've made a good recovery, but it's taken time. And you still have to be careful."

Lady Swynford put up a hand and touched the right side of her face. Her nails were perfect pink ovals against an Elizabeth Arden complexion. "It still shows, doesn't it? Every time I look in the mirror . . ."

"Scarcely at all, and Dr Harvey says it should go away in time."

"If I rest properly. I must do that, he was most insistent. That's why I really can't have the fête here this year. I can't help it if the church roof needs repairing. Surely my health is more important?"

"You won't need to do anything, Mama. I'll cope. I've

always come home for it every year, so I know what happens, and the committee does all the real work anyway."

"Oh, those dreadful committee meetings! I suppose they'll want to hold them here again."

"You don't have to attend them. It isn't necessary."

"I prefer to know what they are proposing to do, thank you, Ruth. I always have attended them and I certainly intend to go on doing so as long as they continue to make use of my property. Last year I had to put a stop to that ridiculous idea of throwing flour bombs at an Aunt Sally. Can you imagine the mess all over the lawn? I insist on being present – *if* I decide to allow them to use the Manor at all. I'll have to think about it." Lady Swynford held out her empty glass. "Get me another one, darling, would you – and stronger this time. The thought of it all is making me feel utterly exhausted."

"I don't know what we're going to do if she says we can't hold it at the Manor."

The Revd William Beede sat down suddenly, as though his legs had given way. He looked and sounded despairing. His wife propelled her wheelchair towards the corner cupboard in the Vicarage sitting-room.

"What you need is a stiff sherry, William. You look tired out and it'll do you good."

"I really shouldn't . . ."

"Nonsense." She had positioned herself deftly alongside the cupboard and was reaching inside for bottle and glasses.

He half rose. "Let me help."

"No need, dear. I can manage perfectly well. You sit there and I'll bring it to you."

She liked to do things herself as much as possible, and so, reluctantly, he stayed where he was while she fumbled with hands that were pitifully clawed and swollen by rheumatoid

## Old Soldiers Never Die

arthritis. For the thousandth time he thought how hard it was sometimes to understand the will of God. Why should He have singled out someone as gentle and harmless and *good* as his wife to bear this pain and suffering. When he was called to the bedside of someone sick or dying who had led a thoroughly selfish and useless life, he was sometimes tempted to feel that they deserved it and that their passing would not exactly deprive the world. But Jean had never harmed a soul in her life and before the cruel disease had virtually crippled her, she had been untiring and selfless in her devotion to all the parish duties that fell to her lot. He could not have wished for a better or more supportive wife, or a more loving one.

She was steering the chair back across the room, balancing the sherry glass carefully. And loved, he thought, watching her, not only by me, but by everyone who knows her. The parishioners had raised the money among themselves to buy her the latest kind of motorised wheelchair. It had given her a wonderful new mobility and independence, enabling her to get about the ground floor of the Vicarage when she was on her own, and, best of all, to keep on with the gardening which was her joy. He had built up the level of the flower beds for her and made special, long-handled tools. Inside the house, he had lowered surfaces and switches and constructed ramps, thanking God that he had been given a talent for DIY, if for little else in life.

"Here you are, dear."

He smiled at her wanly as he took the glass. It was cheap sherry and very sweet, but the parish ladies seem to prefer it like that and so he kept a bottle on hand. It slid stickily down his throat and he repressed a shudder. He positively disliked sherry, but for some reason it was deemed a suitable drink for a Vicar and was always being pressed on him in one form or another. 'A sherry, Vicar?' they would ask, producing anything from Tio Pepe to South African. Whisky and gin were never offered, though he would have infinitely preferred either, and frequently had to watch them being drunk in front of him by everyone else. A brandy would have done the trick better at the moment, he thought, taking another gulp, but they had never been able to afford anything like that.

"I don't know what we're going to do," he repeated, staring down at the glass. "There's nowhere else with a big enough garden – not since the Hall was developed."

"I'm sure Lady Swynford will agree in the end. You mustn't worry, William. It's always been held there, after all."

"That was before she had her stroke."

"She's made a good recovery, though, hasn't she? And Ruth is back now to look after everything."

He gave a helpless shrug. "I should never have *assumed* that it would be all right. It was a bad mistake. I think that's what annoyed her – the assumption that because it had always been so, it would continue for ever. People like Lady Swynford don't like being taken for granted. I should have learnt that by now."

"And people like Lady Swynford enjoy making people dance like puppets, if they think have the power to pull the strings." Jean pressed his arm gently. "They also like to be the centre of attention. I'm quite sure she has no intention of the fête being held anywhere else. She likes playing the role of Lady of the Manor far too much."

Jean had always been a shrewd judge of character, he thought, somewhat comforted. She could see through people and know what they were really like, and what made them so. He had found it tremendously helpful to listen to her wise observations. Many a problem had been solved by following her advice and he had lost count of the arguments averted and impasses resolved at parish council meetings by following her diplomatic recommendations. He put his hand on her misshapen one. "Whatever would I do without you, Jean? Whatever would I do?"

With the aid of her late father's naval binoculars, formerly the property of a German U-boat captain, Freda Butler had watched the removal van disgorging the Colonel's furniture. The sitting-room window of her tiny cottage on the opposite side of the green had an uninterrupted view of most comings and goings and though she was neither a gossip nor a snooper, living alone after a lifetime spent both around and in the Royal Navy had left a gap in her life. She missed the constant human contact and involvement in endless activity. As far as she could, she kept herself busy in village affairs. She was secretary of the local British Legion, as well as of the Frog End Women's Institute; secretary of the garden fête committee; in charge of the Girl Guides; responsible for distribution of the parish magazine; co-ordinator of the neighbourhood watch; and on the church cleaning rota, though not on the one for doing the church flowers – that had never been her forte and there were too many ladies in the village who excelled at the job, in fact, there was cut-throat competition among them for the best arrangements, especially at Christmas and Easter. This Easter, in her opinion, Mrs Grimshaw had won hands down with her font decoration – an exquisitely restrained all-white composition of lilies and narcissi from her own garden and greenhouse that had knocked everyone else's over-filled vases into a cocked hat.

Miss Butler's days were full but her mind still craved added interest. She had watched the Colonel's furniture appearing, piece by piece, and noted its quality. The large sideboard was not dissimilar to the one in her own cottage, left to her by her dear mother – the only good piece, in fact, that she possessed, the rest being mainly junk-shop finds that she had scavenged for when furnishing the cottage on her small savings. If she had not already known from the village grapevine that the newcomer was a retired military man, she would have easily guessed it from his bearing. One glimpse of the tall, erect figure, shoulders back, head held high had told her so. Thirty years in the WRNS had enabled her to spot a military man unerringly. She knew, too, from the grapevine that, like herself, he was alone – though a widower, which would command village respect and sympathy rather than the patronising pity accorded an elderly spinster which was her lot. Still, they were bound to have one thing in common: he, too, would feel the pinch of loneliness and the frustration of inactivity. They would soon be after him, of course, to take on all the jobs nobody else wanted to do: treasurer of the garden fête committee, for example. Since Major Cuthbertson had resigned after three years of rather uncertain office, they had been frantically trying to coerce someone into taking it on. Really, she ought to warn the Colonel but it wasn't her place to do so, and in any case he had the look of someone whom it would not be easy to take advantage of.

While she was watching the unloading she had seen the Vicar coming along in his old Ford and swung her Zeiss binoculars after him, tracking his route as intently as any U-Boat commander after his prey. The car had turned into the Manor gateway. He would be visiting Lady Swynford about the garden fête, and she felt sorry for him to have to creep and crawl to such a person.

Lady Swynford was the kind of woman she most despised, though she kept the fact well concealed. She was self-centred, selfish, arrogant, vain and, as far as Miss Butler could see,

## Old Soldiers Never Die

totally useless to society. Her only contribution to the village community was grudgingly to allow the fête to be held at the Manor once a year. Sir Alan had been quite different when he was alive. He had been chairman of the parish council and of the British Legion, and of the gardening club, and president of the cricket club, involved in all kinds of community affairs. She couldn't understand how he had ever come to marry someone like Lady Swynford. When she had had a stroke soon after Christmas, Miss Butler had had to struggle against feeling rather glad about it; she had even privately refused to add her prayers to those of the Vicar and congregation at matins for Lady Swynford's speedy recovery, keeping her lips tightly closed for the 'Amen'. It had seemed no less than justice for such a selfish existence and for such vanity. Her looks had apparently been seriously marred by the stroke – the right side of her face distorted by paralysis – though when she had finally made a public appearance in the front pew on Easter Sunday everyone could see that it was now barely noticeable. The daughter, Ruth, though, seemed as different from her mother as her father had been. She had unselfishly given up her job in London to come down and look after things, and she was already taking part in local activities – helping on the church cleaning rota and with the church flowers, and was now secretary of the gardening club. She had, obviously, inherited her late father's love of gardening, together with other qualities and attributes.

After the Vicar had passed by, Miss Butler returned to her surveillance of Pond Cottage. Eventually, the removal men came out to close up the lorry tailgate and drive away. They had left the front door open and she saw the moth-eaten-looking tom that had belonged the old Ben appear from nowhere and saunter in, bold as brass. How uncanny cats were! He'd been missing for weeks but must have known somehow that his adopted home was ready for occupation again. She waited, with interest, to see if the Colonel ejected him but nothing happened and, presently, she saw Mrs Grimshaw leave Pear Tree Cottage next door and stride round to her new neighbour's gate.

She liked Naomi Grimshaw. She was one of the very few people in the village who did not patronise or pity her for her unmarried state. In fact, if anything, she seemed to applaud it. Her own marriage, she rather gathered, had been less than satisfactory – the precise details shrouded, not exactly in mystery but in vagueness. The husband was long dead, rather conveniently, she suspected, which was why Mrs Grimshaw had come back to live with her sister at the Hall, until they had sold to the developer and bought Pear Tree Cottage. It was sad that Miss Gurney had died so soon afterwards, just when they were comfortably re-settled there. She had been a kind, gentle sort of person – unmarried, of course, like herself, but according to village gossip she had once been engaged to Sir Alan Swynford, until the present Lady Swynford had appeared on the scene and the engagement had been broken off. It was also common knowledge that there was no love lost between Mrs Grimshaw and her sister's supplanter, even though it had all happened a long time ago. The sparks always flew at any encounter, and would be bound to fly again at the forthcoming garden fête committee meeting. In fact, there was always a good deal of argument all round. As secretary, Miss Butler was not particularly looking forward to the job of recording the minutes accurately but in a form that would give no offence to anybody when she finally had to read them out.

Mrs Grimshaw had waited a moment at the front door of Pond Cottage and then boldly gone in through the open doorway, like the cat. She wondered what the Colonel would

## Old Soldiers Never Die

make of her forthright way of speaking, not to mention her way of dressing. Miss Butler herself wore calf-length skirts, blouses and cardigans, lisle stockings and low-heeled lace-up shoes, not so very different from the naval uniform that she had worn for so long. Each to his or her own, as she frequently told herself. The world would be a dull place if everyone was the same.

Mrs Grimshaw did not reappear, so presumably she and the Colonel were talking. She was probably telling him about the village, perhaps even mentioning herself. Miss Butler lives in Lupin Cottage – that little one across the green with the bay window and the yellow door. She comes from a naval family. Her father was an admiral, you know.

She lowered the glasses which were making her arms ache. The studio photograph of Father in full dress uniform stood close by her on the top of the bureau, the double row of medals prominently lit. He was staring directly at the camera with that stern expression, tinged with impatience, she had known so well. Miss Butler fully realised that she had been something of a disappointment to her father. In the first place she had not been a son, and in the second, when she had tried to make up for this by joining the only branch of the navy open to her, she had not risen as high in the service as he had expected of her. She had enjoyed her modestly successful career in administration: she liked the order and neatness of the rules and regulations that seemed irksome to many. She had been punctilious in her duties, conscientious over all responsibilities, and utterly reliable, but somehow she had lacked the ambitious drive and personality that had taken other WRN officers towards the top. Whenever she looked at the photograph of her father, as now, she was reminded of it.

The shadows were lengthening across the village green, the sun dipping gradually lower; from the settled sky it looked as though it would be another fine day tomorrow. She would make an early start, delivering the new parish magazines, and in the evening there was a neighbourhood watch meeting to attend. There had been two burglaries in the village recently and extra vigilance was needed; a police officer from Dorchester was coming to advise. Next week it would be the annual Red Cross door-to-door collection again. How the years went by! Faster and faster.

The clock on the mantlepiece chimed seven. She put the binoculars carefully away in their hiding place in the bureau. Time to prepare herself a light supper, a poached egg on toast perhaps or a sardine salad. Not very exciting but it would have to do. Miss Butler moved towards her little kitchen at the back of the cottage.

Upstairs in her bedroom, Ruth Swynford looked at herself in the dressing-table mirror. She picked up her brush and dragged it quickly through her hair and then put it down again. Extraordinary how she simply didn't care any longer what she looked like. The personal assistant in tailored career suit and blouse, well-cut hair, careful make-up, discreet spray of Miss Dior, had completely vanished. Her hair was a mess, so were her hands and nails, and the clothes she put on in the morning were whatever would be both practical and comfortable for working in the garden. She no longer bothered with make-up or scent.

She wondered what Ralph would make of this metamorphosis and the thought made her smile dryly at her reflection. If he could see her now, he'd probably say to himself, 'thank God I had the sense to end it'. And he'd probably be right.

Eight years – that was how long their affair had lasted. Eight years of deception and pretence and self-delusion, of all the classic ingredients of a boss–secretary liaison. Eight years,

## Old Soldiers Never Die

for Ralph, of lying to his wife, and eight years for her of lonely weekends and evenings in her mansion flat, interspersed with the ones they somehow contrived to spend together and which made up for all the others. 'It won't be like this for ever, Ruth, I swear it. I'll speak to Helen soon. Tell her I want a divorce. Just as soon as the time is right . . .'

But the time had somehow never been right. Other circumstances had always intervened: his son's Common Entrance, his daughter's O levels, his son's confirmation, his own promotion to managing director, his daughter's wedding, his mother's long illness. 'It would kill Mother to hear about us, Ruth. You know what that generation are like. Marriage is for keeps with them. I can't do that to her at the moment.' But when his mother had finally died, there was something else that made it impossible for him to leave his wife. She'd forgotten precisely what . . . something to do with selling their house and moving to the country. It didn't really matter what it was because, like all the other reasons it had only been an excuse. The mystery, looking back, was how on earth she had deluded herself for so long; how she had kept up her hopes so pathetically for eight weary years, until the final evening at her flat when Ralph had had the sense to end it. 'I'm sorry, Ruth, but I think it's time we stopped seeing each other . . . better for both of us in the long run . . . it's not fair on you . . . you're bound to meet someone else, get married yourself.'

Of course, she had protested that she didn't want to do anything of the kind, that she didn't mind so long as she could go on seeing him, that she couldn't bear not to. On and on, she'd gone and how she must have irritated him with her pleading and her snivelling! He had listened in silence and then he had told her that his daughter was having a baby and if he were to get divorced he would risk not being able to see his grandchild. Watching his set face, as he trotted out yet another excuse, she had realised with horrible clarity that he had never wanted to leave his wife, and had never had any intention of doing so. His family meant far more to him than she had ever done and she had been too blind to see it: blind with love, and there was nothing blinder. It still hurt appallingly if she was careless enough to let herself think of him. But she couldn't blame him. She could only blame herself for being so stupid for so long.

She turned away from the mirror and went to close the window against the cool of the evening. Her bedroom overlooked the big lawn at the back of the house and she could see the whole length of the herbaceous border. She stood for a moment, considering it, noting the gaps, thinking what changes might be made. She ought to take out the boring old red hot pokers that had been there for years and plant something else . . . delphiniums, perhaps. Some of the ones with the lovely names she'd been reading about: 'Blue Jade', 'Belladonna', 'Bluebird'. She'd chosen some of the new plants in the garden for their name alone, especially the roses: 'Danse du Feu', 'Golden Showers', 'Comtesse de Murinais', 'Fragrant Cloud', 'Compassion'. Dephiniums would be more work with all the staking but it would be worth it. Delphiniums blue and geraniums red, like the old rhyme. She had already planted geraniums red, not the shrieking garden-centre scarlet of the modern kind but soft pink and red, good old-fashioned cranesbills. Her eye moved on. Out with the globe thistles that had rampaged around at the back of the far end for years! In with some kind of mallow or hollyhocks, or maybe euphorbia, if it grew tall enough. She must ask Naomi Grimshaw's advice. There was plenty of room in that gap in the middle for another peony . . . a double white one, perhaps: 'Alba Plena', or the rose-red 'Felix Crousse'. She was learning slowly, as she went along, and how strange it was that she

## Old Soldiers Never Die

should have conceived this passion for gardening so unexpectedly when she had never taken the slightest interest before. Not until she had come back from London to look after Mama. Wandering miserably around, thinking of Ralph, she had eventually noticed how neglected the gardens had become. When Pa had been alive they had been his pride and joy; he had worked in them himself, together with old Mr Bean, digging and weeding and hoeing and pruning and planting. Mama had never lifted a trowel in her life and was only interested in there being perfect flowers available when it came round to her turn to do the church arrangements: the source of a long-running battle between herself and Mr Bean. Since Pa had died the old gardener had retired and a succession of young ones had come and gone, all useless so far as she had been able to see from the overgrown shrubs, the unpruned roses and messy borders. With time on her hands while her mother was resting during her convalescence, she had decided to do something about it and rolled up her sleeves and set to work. In the space of months, that impulse had grown almost into an obsession. She had devoured all her father's old gardening books and bought new ones from the bookshop in Dorchester, and worked long hours out of doors and in the greenhouse. And she had hired a new gardener to help her.

On cue, as she thought about him, Jacob appeared at the far end of the lawn, trundling a wheelbarrow along the path that led to the compost heap. He was working late, as usual, but there was nothing she could do to stop him; he was one of those people who seem to belong to the soil and the land rather than to the human race. And, anyway, what was the alternative? For him to spend the evening all alone in his bed-sitting-room in the old stable block? He never went down to the Dog and Duck or into Dorchester, so far as she knew. She had no idea how he passed his leisure time; she had only ever seen him working. Jacob was a curiously bibilical name for someone like him. She had often wondered why he had been called that and where he had come from. He had just turned up at the Manor one day, asking for work – like a stray animal in search of a kindly home.

She watched him as he loped along the path with his strange, jerky, gait, shoulders stooped, long thin arms stuck out like a scarecrow's to the barrow's handles, the floppy canvas hat he always wore, shielding the upper part of his face. His head made a curious pecking movement forward, like a chicken. Poor Jacob! Even at this distance, it was obvious that he was a bit odd, not barmy, exactly, but uncoordinated, clumsy – except with plants – painfully shy and inarticulate to the point of dumbness. Mama couldn't stand him and would have sacked him on the spot when she'd first set eyes on him, if Ruth hadn't pointed out how hard it was to get help these days and what a disgrace the garden was. Mama minded about her Lady of the Manor status, almost as much as she minded about her looks, and so Jacob had been allowed to stay, so long as he kept out of her way. He seemed to do so instinctively, scuttling away the instant her mother appeared.

Ruth watched him disappear round the corner and then looked at her watch, half past seven. Downstairs, in the kitchen, Mrs Hunt would be dishing up the dinner. Once, long ago, and before her time, the Manor would have had a full staff – cook, butler, maids, chauffeur, gardeners – now there was only Mrs Hunt who came in the evenings and Mrs Cousins who obliged on Tuesdays and Fridays. Time to go down and brave Mrs Hunt's Dorset version of chile con carne.

# Three

Over the next few days, the Colonel made a start with some of the removal boxes. He put away china and glass, arranged books on shelves and hung pictures on walls, hammering in hooks randomly. Laura, he knew, would have taken time and trouble with the pictures and he would have been holding each in turn against the wall, while she stood back to see the effect. "Up a bit, Hugh, could you? No, that's too high. A bit lower, and to the left . . ."

The effort expended to get it all just right used to exasperate him sometimes; now he missed the little ritual terribly.

One box contained all the framed family photographs, each shrouded in newspaper, and he took them out, one by one, unwrapping them and dusting the glass with the sleeve of his jacket. First the old velvet-framed black and white studio portrait of his mother in thirties evening dress and pearls, then the one of his father – ramrod straight in his army uniform. He set them together on the sofa table nearby. Both of them had been dead for more than fifteen years but the memory of them was still fresh in his mind. They had been good and affectionate parents and had given him the priceless gift of a happy, secure childhood. He unwrapped the next one which tugged no heart-strings. It was the one of his late mother-in-law. The mystery, to him, had always been how she had produced a daughter like Laura, and he had not been able to mourn her passing one jot. She'd been a discontented and thoroughly difficult woman and one advantage of their nomadic army life had been seeing her very little. He put the photograph in its expensive frame away at the back of a drawer.

He was about to take out the next when there was a ring at the front door. It was the second caller that morning – the first had been another retired army officer, somewhat older than himself, who had wanted him to be treasurer of some committee for a summer fête. He might as well make himself useful as soon as possible, though he had no experience of village fêtes and had said so. Major Cuthbertson had explained blithely that it didn't matter in the least. The only requirement, apparently, was that it should be someone they could trust not to fiddle the books or run off with the takings. "Only a few hundred pounds, of course," he'd added, with a bark of a laugh. "Wouldn't get anyone very far these days, what?"

His second visitor was female and also of retirement age. He looked at the slight, grey-haired figure, neatly dressed in navy skirt and cardigan, and wondered what she wanted of him. Then she proffered a cardboard box and a tin and he saw that she was collecting for the Red Cross: a good cause, if ever there was one. He smiled at her and said so. She had the apologetic look of the collector who is not sure of a good reception.

"My wallet's upstairs. If you wouldn't mind waiting a moment . . ." He saw that she was trying to see into the hallway behind him. "Please come in, if you would like."

She advanced with her box and tin. "Perhaps I will. Quite a cool breeze today. Very chilly, first thing. We're not into summer yet, are we?"

"No, indeed."

He showed her into the sitting-room. "Please sit down. I won't keep you long."

## Old Soldiers Never Die

He went upstairs for his wallet and when he came down she was sitting on the very edge of the tapestry chair, feet neatly together, the tin and box on her lap. He folded a five pound note and put it into the slot.

"How *very* generous, Colonel..."

"Not at all. The Red Cross does wonderful work. They deserve every penny."

"I so agree with you! But many people don't seem to feel that. It's quite surprising how those that can afford the most often give the least. Some even hide and pretend they're out. Of course, there are so many collections these days that I suppose you can't blame them."

She thrust the box at him and he took a sticker for his lapel.

"Can I offer you some coffee. Or a cup of tea, perhaps?"

She shook her head quite vehemently. "Oh, no, I shouldn't dream of troubling you, Colonel. Thank you so much. If you don't mind my saying, I think your cottage looks very nice."

"Thank you. I'm afraid I'm not much good at interiors. My wife was the one who always coped with that."

"Yes, of course. I'm so sorry..." Her voice trailed away, embarrassed. "It must be very difficult for you. I've never been married, so I'm rather used to fending for myself. Like you, I was in the services. I was in the WRNS for thirty years. I must say I do miss it."

He smiled sympathetically. "I miss the army, too. They retire us service people much too young, don't they?"

He knew she must be quite a bit older than he was – probably close to seventy – but what woman minds being thought of as younger than she is? He saw a faint flush creep across her cheeks and knew he had said the right thing. Ironically, she immediately *did* look younger.

"My father certainly found retirement very... difficult. He was an admiral, you see."

He looked suitably impressed. "Really? That must have been a hard adjustment for him."

She nodded. "Yes, it was. He became very depressed. Quite at a loose end."

He could imagine all too easily. It was the typical problem of the powerful and important suddenly left powerless and of importance no more.

She stood up. "Well, I must be getting along, I'm only halfway round the village. It's been very nice meeting you, Colonel."

He conducted her to the door. "You haven't told me your name."

The flush deepened. "How silly of me! It's Miss Butler. Freda Butler." She shook his hand. "I hope you'll be very happy here, Colonel."

He waited politely until she had closed the gate and gone on her way with a quick little wave of her hand, and then went back to his unpacking.

The next photograph was of Alison. It had been taken some time ago to mark her twenty-first birthday and the London photographer had done a good job. He considered it for a moment, seeing in the large eyes and the small, straight nose her resemblance to Laura. It was a physical resemblance only: in character she was very different. An independent, self-sufficient, career woman – a top executive in the London offices of an American PR company. If there was a serious boyfriend he didn't know of him – nobody shared her Chelsea flat, so far as he was aware. She had been a lively, spirited, amusing child who had grown into an affectionate and interesting daughter; he liked and admired her, as well as loving her dearly. He put the photograph on his desk.

The photographer at Marcus and Susan's wedding had been less successful. To be fair, it had poured with rain and the

## Old Soldiers Never Die

light had been poor, but when he unwrapped the picture of the bridal pair taken at the church door, it brought back all the disappointment he had privately felt on that day. It would have been quite unreasonable to have expected his daughter-in-law to be a raving beauty, and Susan was perfectly nice-looking, even in that unfortunate frilly creation she'd worn, but he had not been prepared for her to be so *dull*. He would far sooner that she had been ugly rather than boring, though he knew how unjust he was being. She was a good mother to Eric, born eight years later, and she kept the house in Leicester immaculately clean and tidy, but he had never heard her make any sort of joke. He had once admitted to Laura that he found Susan dull and humourless and she had remarked, quite rightly, that since he wasn't married to her it shouldn't worry him. Besides, as Laura had also pointed out, Marcus seemed perfectly happy with her and that was all that mattered. He had been a quiet, steady sort of boy and after Charterhouse and Exeter he had found a steady management job with a big frozen food firm in the Midlands. He put the photograph on his desk, close to Alison's.

Now he had come to the two that he dreaded. He knew which was which by their size and shape: first, the blue leather double folder of the engagement photos by Baron – Laura on the left, himself on the right; then their own wedding photo in a silver frame, taken on a gloriously sunny summer's day thirty-nine years ago. He forced himself to unwrap both and to look at them, to face the past, fair and square.

How incredibly young they both looked. And how incredibly beautiful Laura had been. He thought of their first meeting at a rather dull army party given by a senior officer when he had been a young subaltern. He'd been awkward and ill-at-ease, he remembered, fumbling with cigarette and glass, and not knowing what to do with either when it came to shaking hands. Laura had been staying with her older married sister whose husband was also in the army. He had seen her from across the room and she had been surrounded by other young subalterns and was obviously enjoying herself in their company. It was her sister, Pat, whom he knew slightly, who had extricated her and brought her across. Years later, when he asked Pat why, she had smiled and said simply that she had known they were right for each other.

He was lost in more memories when the door bell rang again, bringing him sharply back to the present. He went to answer it. Naomi Grimshaw stood before him, holding something in her hand as Miss Butler had done, but in this case it was a jam jar. Her purple jogging suit seared his eyeballs.

She waved the jar at him. "Brought you some home-made chutney, Hugh. Last year's, of course, but it should be all right."

"How kind of you."

He made the mistake of standing back and she was through the door and past him in a flash.

"I'll put it in the kitchen, shall I? It'll come in useful with cold meat, and things."

He followed her into the kitchen – she knew exactly where that was – and she put the jar down on a counter, looking round with approval.

"You've done a good job in here, too. I'd never've recognised it. See you've kept the old range."

"Only for show. I rather liked it."

She nodded agreement. "Nice old thing. Looks wonderful now. They don't make them like that any more. It's probably fifty years old at least. Nowadays things are only meant to last five, then you throw them away and pay out another fortune for a new one. Can you cook?"

"I can heat things up."

"You must learn properly, Hugh. I'm not much good myself, but that's one thing to avoid when you live alone – heating things up out of tins or having those frightful ready-made meals. No proper nourishment for you at all. I'll write down some simple recipes for you to try, if you like."

"Thank you." Anything to humour her, he thought.

"Is that your wedding picture?"

He realised that he was still holding it in one hand.

"Mind if I look?" She took it from him. Her spectacles were dangling from a cord round her neck and she propped them on the end of her nose, and studied the black and white photo for a moment in silence. Then she gave it back. "I can see why you miss her so much."

"I'm sure you must miss your husband."

"No, I don't. Not a bit. He was a bastard. And a mean old skinflint, too. He went off with his secretary in the end, much to my relief."

"I thought you were widowed."

"I am now. I'm a widowed divorcee, if that's possible. He died five years ago, but we were divorced before that. I've always said I'm widowed because it sounds so much better. Specially round here. Widows have a far better image than divorcees, don't they? Same applies to widowers."

She gave him a cheery smile and he returned it, amused. Then and there he decided that he liked Naomi Grimshaw.

She moved to peer out of the window. "Done anything to the garden?"

"Not a thing yet. It's a jungle."

"Let's take a look. I could help, maybe."

He led the way out through the scullery and the back door where they were confronted by a tangled and flourishing mass of nettles and brambles. Naomi, nothing daunted, picked up a large stick conveniently to hand and laid about her, stomping a pathway under her big white trainers. Beyond, as he already knew from his first winter inspection with the agent, and from looking out of the upstairs windows, were the remnants of a lawn, a hopelessly overgrown flower bed, some shrubs – either out of control or struggling for survival – a tree or two and everywhere rampant and ferocious brambles. He followed, reluctantly, in Naomi's enthusiastic wake; it seemed even worse than he had thought, or remembered, presumably because everything was now growing fast.

He stood, watching, while she beat about her with the stick, prodding and poking in various corners, then she disappeared from his view. He could hear her thrashing around energetically and Thursday, obviously disturbed in some favourite sleeping spot, emerged from the undergrowth and stalked past huffily.

After a while, Naomi returned to his side with the light of a challenge glinting in her eyes. "Bit of a mess, it must be said. But nothing that can't be dealt with. Good clear out of all the muck. Good cutting back. Kill off the nettles. Out with all the old rubbishy stuff and in with some new. You won't know it by the end of the summer." She waved the stick at him. "Planning, that's the secret. Pencil and paper. Work it out. Trial and error, of course, but that's the nice thing about gardening. You can correct your mistakes. If a plant won't grow somewhere, haul it out and stuff it somewhere else. If you decide you don't like it, give it away to someone who does. Now, you've already got the basics in place here."

He looked round at the wilderness. "Have I?"

"Rather! Two nice old apple trees at the far end, for a start, still fruiting well, by the looks of them. A plum tree and a beautiful white lilac, don't know how *that* got there. Trees are important, as I'm sure you'll agree?"

"Well, yes. I suppose they are."

## Old Soldiers Never Die

"Framework, you see. Shade, too. So, you want to keep those. Then you've got a good strong honeysuckle by the wall and a healthy-looking rambler, all they need is cutting back, and I spotted some nice iris coming along in that damp corner. And you've got some some good cottage perennials in the bed – delphiniums, poppies, lupins . . . She looked round, nodding. "It's a pretty garden, though you can't see it now. Old Ben used to keep it in order, once upon a time. Then of course he got too old and stopped caring."

"I was wondering if *I* cared that much," he said mildly, realising that, as a gardener, he might fall somewhat short of her expectations.

"Of course you care!" she said firmly. "Gardening is balm to the soul, as well as one of life's most creative activities. I recommend it very strongly to someone in your situation. And plants are friends, you know. You can talk to them."

"And do they answer?" he asked, smiling.

"They answer by growing, or not growing. If they don't grow then they're telling you something's wrong. I don't know why people are so rude about poor Prince Charles talking to his plants. It seems quite normal to me. All good gardeners do it."

"I'm afraid I'm not really a gardener at all. I've never owned a garden in my life, or worked in one."

She waved the stick at him again. "Well, now's the time to start, Hugh. Mind you, I think you'll need some help, getting this lot cleared. Some strong young man – and there aren't many of those in Frog End. Tell you what, I'll ask Jacob, the gardener, up at the Manor. He might give you a hand an evening or two. He's a bit odd, but he's got real green fingers."

"Wouldn't his employers mind?"

"Ursula Swynford would mind about anything that didn't benefit her, but I don't see how she could actually object if it was in his time off. Ruth wouldn't mind a bit – that's the Swynford daughter. She's getting to be a pretty good gardener, too now, since she came home. Funny how it can catch up with you in life. Want me to ask Jacob? As I say, he's a bit of an odd one, so it'd better come from me. If he sees anyone he doesn't know he just beetles off, or hides."

The glint was still in her eye and he saw that it would be hopeless to prevaricate. "All right, thanks, Naomi. I'd be very grateful."

They went back into the cottage, retracing the beaten path.

"I hear old Roger Cuthbertson press-ganged you onto the garden fête committee as treasurer." Naomi said as they reached the hall.

"News travels fast."

"Met him in the village shop after he'd called on you this morning. Silly old buffer, waffling on, as usual. Pity I didn't warn you he'd try that. He was desperate to unload the job onto somebody."

"Oh, I don't mind too much. I've plenty of time at the moment."

"Wait till you've sat through our committee meetings and spent a hot Saturday afternoon counting up eight hundred pounds odd in five and two pence pieces. I do the plant stall – more fool me. Did Roger tell you there's a meeting this Friday? Eleven a.m. at the Manor?"

"Yes, I gather so."

She gave him a dry smile. "You'll meet more of our fascinating Frog End residents then, including our Lady of the Manor."

He opened the door for her. "I'll look forward to it."

He watched her stride away briskly, without any backward glance or little wave like his previous visitor. When she went, Naomi Grimshaw went.

## Old Soldiers Never Die

Later, when he picked up the jar from the counter, he read the bold handwriting on the label: Tomatoe Chutney. He smiled to himself. She couldn't spell quite as well as she could garden.

"What's he like?"

Major Cuthbertson grunted. "Seems nice enough. Typical army type. Pretty sound. Anyway, he's taking on the job of treasurer, thank God. Didn't take much persuading."

Marjorie Cuthbertson smiled grimly. "Lucky you got to him when you did, before anyone else could put him off."

She dished up the re-heated stew and they sat down to lunch in the bungalow dining room. In spite of the sunny spring day she wore a thick tweed skirt and a lambswool twinset and, under that, a thermal vest. Much of the Major's army service had been abroad in hotter places and she always maintained that she had never re-adapted properly to the English climate.

"We never came across him, did we?"

Her husband removed a piece of gristle from his mouth to the side of his plate before answering. "Don't think so. Different regiment, of course."

Unspoken between them was also the difference in rank. Both had been deeply disappointed that after a lifetime's service the Major had only risen thus far. There were times when Mrs Cuthbertson, daughter of a major general, privately felt that she could have done considerably better for herself – a view her late parents had also shared. She got round the problem chiefly by ignoring it and by deploying her natural authority. Among a number of suitable local responsibilities, she was chairman of the garden fête committee.

"Did you tell him about the meeting on Friday?"

The Major nodded, chewing hard; he had encountered

another piece of gristle. Damn it, the teeth wouldn't take it these days. He took a gulp of water.

"Eleven o'clock. The Manor. He knows."

"I hope he's punctual. We've got a great deal to get through. You'll be there too, of course."

"Well, I thought as I won't be treasurer any longer –"

"Fortunately. Finance has never been your forte, Roger, nor even simple arithmetic. I can't think why you took the job on in the first place. I should never have let you. However, be that as it may, you've got to do *something*, so you must certainly be there. I know, you can be in charge of the bottle stall this year." Marjorie Cuthbertson paused and added with dry significance. "*That* ought to suit you."

# Four

Frog End Manor was a Jacobean house built in local stone and shielded from the villagers' impertinent gaze by a high wall completely encircling the grounds.

When the Colonel arrived for the garden fête committee meeting, there were other cars already parked on the gravel sweep and he found a space for his beside the red Metro that he recognised as Naomi Grimshaw's. As he walked up to the front door, he admired the beauty and rich antiquity of the house: the mellow stone, the mullioned windows, the serene air of belonging completely to its surroundings and of having done so for more than three hundred years. The surrounding trees were mature, some perhaps more than a hundred of those years old, and the gnarled and twisted wisteria clambering across the front of the house, and now in glorious purple bloom, had obviously been doing so for many a spring.

The door had been left open and, after a moment's hesitation, he walked into the hall, his eyes adjusting from bright sunlight to the dimness of an oak-panelled interior. A small black French poodle came trotting towards him across the flagstone floor, giving shrill little yaps. Its curly coat had been shorn on the body and clipped and teased on head and legs and tail into fluffy pom-poms, like canine topiary. He noticed with distaste that its collar was studded with jewel-coloured stones. Wrong sort of dog entirely, he thought. It should be a wolfhound or a setter, or a labrador: something appropriate to an English country house, not to the boulevards of Paris.

He could hear voices coming from an open doorway at the far end of the hall and went towards them, the poodle prancing along before him, yapping. As he did so a young woman emerged. She smiled at him and held out her hand. "I'm Ruth Swynford. Do come on in, Colonel."

Everyone in the village seemed to know who he was, even though he was still in the dark about most of them. This must be the daughter of the house, the one recently returned home of whom Naomi had spoken. She was dressed in cord slacks and a blue cotton shirt and her face was suntanned and free of any make-up. A keen gardener, Naomi had said, but surely not the owner of the poodle? The dog was still jumping about his ankles and yapping at him as he followed her into the room, almost tripping him up.

"Sorry about Shoo-Shoo." Ruth Swynford said. "It's because he doesn't know you. He's fine once he does." She grabbed hold of the jewelled collar and pulled the poodle away. "Have you met everybody yet?"

He looked at the members of the garden fête Committee who were standing around in a group in the centre of the drawing-room, all heads turned towards him at his noisy entrance. Naomi (in an emerald-green tracksuit today) shouted out "Morning, Hugh," and Miss Butler, standing beside Major Cuthbertson, gave him a timid smile. The rest were strangers to him.

The Major stepped forward, as though he felt some responsibility for the situation, and introduced the Colonel to his wife who was apparently the committee chairman. Mrs Cuthbertson, dressed in lambswool and thick tweeds, looked as though she would have no trouble controlling the proceedings. She was a big woman, like Naomi, and about the same age, but whereas he would apply the word statuesque to his next-door neighbour, solid was the one that came to mind for Mrs Cuthbertson. She was constructed along the lines of a battleship with a pronounced prow and a large stern. Her voice was ringingly county.

"How do you do, Colonel. And welcome."

She might have been the lady of the house greeting him in her own drawing-room. Where, he wondered, was Lady Swynford?

More introductions were made by Mrs Cuthbertson who had now swept her husband aside.

"Mrs Grimshaw, you already know, I gather, she's the plant stall. This is Miss Butler, our secretary."

"Miss Butler and I have already met, too." He returned another timid smile.

"Oh, really?" Mrs Cuthbertson, surprised, moved on. "Miss Rankin who does our pony rides."

Miss Rankin wiped her hand down the side of her jodphurs before offering it to him. She was somewhere in her fifties he gauged, with a weatherbeaten face and red Dutch-doll patches of broken veins on her cheeks. There was a stray piece of straw on the sleeve of her green jumper and a faint but unmistakable aroma of horse manure about her.

"Mrs Bentley and Mrs Thompson, cake stall. Mrs Warner, bric-a-brac, Mr Townsend, hoop-la, Mrs Latimer, books, Mrs Fox, teas . . ."

He moved round around the circle, shaking hands and smiling. They all eyed him with curiosity – not in an unfriendly way, but holding judgement in reserve. It was rather like being a new boy at school and facing the upper fourth.

"Our Vicar, Mr Beede, of course. No doubt he's already called on you."

The Vicar, standing diffidently at the very edge of the

gathering, flushed above his dog collar. His grey hair looked at odds with a still youthful face.

"Unfortunately, not. Do forgive me, Colonel. I've been so busy lately. Of course, I intended to do so at the earliest opportunity –"

"Delighted to meet you, Vicar."

He shook his hand heartily. Padres had always made him feel slightly uncomfortable. He didn't really belong to their club and there was an added awkwardness now with this one. Vicars, he knew, were supposed to call on new parishioners, but, personally, the Colonel was thankful he hadn't though he could hardly say so. Mrs Cuthbertson was giving the wretched man a withering look and started to say something to him when someone else entered the drawing-room and the gathering fell silent.

It was very obviously Lady Swynford. She stood just inside the doorway, holding the theatrical pose of a star pausing to await the audience's acclaim. She even carried some kind of silken scarf in one hand, the standard leading lady's prop from old drawing-room comedies; he could remember seeing Evelyn Laye trailing one about. All eyes were upon her and the Colonel observed the various reactions with interest. The Vicar's flush had turned to pallor and the Major was fingering his bow tie like a nervous swain. Others, including Mrs Cuthbertson, had switched on fawning smiles. On Freda Butler's innocuous face, though, he was somewhat surprised to see an expression of contempt, almost hatred. Naomi, seemed to have gained in size: her chest swelled like a pouter pigeon's with an exasperated intake of breath. Lady Swynford's daughter, Ruth, was watching her mother in a detached, expressionless way as though she had seen the performance many times before.

The silence was broken by the Major who hurried forward

## Old Soldiers Never Die

offering to arrange a chair for her. Lady Swynford waved him away.

"I shall sit in my usual place. You know I never like to interfere."

The Colonel heard Naomi say, "Not much!"

Lady Swynford had sunk onto a Hepplewhite chair near the door, distancing herself pointedly from the committee. The poodle jumped up onto her lap and she caressed its ears. The scarf fluttered like a starter's flag. "Do begin."

They sat down in a rough circle round the room with Mrs Cuthbertson presiding at the twelve o'clock position, a small table before her. The minutes of the previous meeting were read by Miss Butler, approved after some minor quibbling and signed. The Major proposed the Colonel's election as the new Treasurer and was instantly seconded as though they were afraid he might change his mind if he got the chance. Mrs Cuthbertson welcomed him graciously to the committee.

He listened with half an ear as the next item on the agenda was discussed, taking in his surroundings. As in the hall, the walls were panelled and the open fireplace could have roasted a very large sheep, if not quite an ox. It was a lovely room furnished with appropriately fine antiques and paintings. Laura, he knew, would have admired it greatly. If she had lived, she might have been sitting where he was now as a new committee member, running some kind of stall. She would have enjoyed that. It would have been part of the putting-down-roots-in-England process that she had looked forward to for so long.

"What do you think, Colonel?"

Mrs Cuthbertson was looking in his direction, tapping her pencil on the table.

"I'm sorry?"

"About the entrance price. Do you think it should be raised?"

He had no idea from what to what. He had been miles away, thinking about Laura but some answer was required of him.

"On the whole, no. It would probably be better to concentrate on persuading people to spend more once they're in."

The Major nodded in emphatic agreement and so did several others. He seemed to have said the right thing.

The morning wore on. Every so often Lady Swynford interrupted the proceedings with some proviso: there were to be no stakes driven into the lawn, no stalls up on the terrace, the croquet lawn was to be roped off and out of bounds, and a proposal for a children's small pet show was quashed immediately. Mrs Latimer, who had put forward the suggestion, made a brave attempt to save it.

"Just *small* pets, Lady Swynford – guinea pigs, tortoises, hamsters, white mice, goldfish . . ."

"They could get out and do untold damage in the gardens."

Naomi said caustically. "Goldfish would hardly leap out of their bowls, Ursula. And the kids would love it."

"The others could get out, though. They'd bring them in shoe boxes and flimsy things like that. I really couldn't allow it. Besides, there's the mess – straw everywhere."

"We'd clear up any mess."

"Like the ice-cream wrappers we were picking up for weeks afterwards last year? I certainly hope you're not intending to sell ice creams again. People seem to forget that this is private property, they behave as though they were at Blackpool."

The individual stalls were discussed in detail, and the number of trestle tables required by each. As only twenty-four were available from the village-hall store there was fierce competition.

## Old Soldiers Never Die

Mrs Bentley of the cake stall put up her hand. "If I may speak, Madam Chairman. Mrs Thompson and I can't possibly manage with less than three. As everybody knows cakes are the most popular stall and we get a lot of contributions. There's always a big rush—"

"The bottle stall's pretty popular, too," the Major commented loudly enough for everyone to hear. "Bigger draw than cakes any day, I'd say."

Mrs Bentley glared at him. "I don't think so, Major And, personally, I don't approve of us having a bottle stall at all. I don't think drinking should be actively encouraged."

"Eating cakes can be just as bad for you," he countered stubbornly. "Cholesterol and all that sort of thing . . . clots the arteries. They say alcohol actually *thins* the blood, you know, there was a big article about it in the newspapers—"

His wife cut the argument short before it could escalate, adjudicating between them like Solomon. Three tables for the cake stall, *one* only for bottle stall. The Major went on muttering to himself.

Miss Rankin had stuck up her hand. "Sorry, but I can only bring two ponies this year. Just thought I'd tell you now, Madam Chairman."

"You usually provide four, Miss Rankin."

"Molly's gone lame on me and Hector's getting too old. It takes it out of them you know, having all those children bumping around on their backs and pulling at their mouths."

"Surely they're used to that at your riding school?"

"My pupils are properly instructed with a course of lessons. I can't do that in a five-minute pony ride with a long queue of the little perishers. Some of the boys think they're Clint Eastwood out in the Wild West."

"Oh, I always think he rides rather nicely," Mrs Warner of bric-a-brac had spoken up. She was wearing a flowered cotton frock that reached to thick ankles and her wispy hair was screwed up in a tight knot on the top of her head.

"Roy Rogers, then," Miss Rankin said impatiently. "You know what I mean, tearing about all over the place."

"Actually, *he* used to sing quite a lot."

"That was Gene Autry."

"Roy Rogers did too. He was a sort of gentleman cowboy."

"Well, Hopalong Cassidy, then. The Lone Ranger—"

Mrs Cuthbertson tapped the end of her pencil sharply on the table. "Keep to the point, please. If you can only manage two ponies, Miss Rankin, then I suppose we'll have to make do with that this year. Takings will be down, of course. We'll have to make it up in other areas. How about teas, Mrs Fox? Can you do better there?"

"Better?" Mrs Fox looked indignant. "We did nearly two hundred of them last year. Besides, we've only so many cups and saucers and people don't always bring them back to be washed up. Six got broken, too. We had to replace them, of course, because they belong to the WI."

Mrs Warner put up her hand again. "May I propose, Madam Chairman, that we buy some more cups and saucers out of our reserve and keep them for our own use? Then we could sell more teas?"

Mrs Fox rounded on her. "You can't get the same pattern. It's discontinued. We got the last six in stock."

"Surely they don't have to match? We could get something similar. Mine at home are quite like it, only they've got more flowers on them. You can get them in Dorchester. And they're dishwasher safe."

"We don't use a dishwasher," Mrs Fox said coldly. "We wash everything up ourselves, by hand. Anyway, I'm not in favour of mixing china. It looks slapdash, to my way of thinking."

## Old Soldiers Never Die

The Colonel rested his chin on his hand. What was he doing here, wasting the morning listening to arguments over cowboys and teacups? Had his life really come down to this? Naomi Grimshaw, seated opposite, caught his eye and raised hers heavenwards.

Mrs Cuthbertson tapped her pencil again. "Next item. Wet weather contingency plans."

A frisson passed round the room, like a wind blowing through long grass.

She ploughed on grimly. "Last year we were lucky, but we can't count on the same this year." She paused. "I wonder if Lady Swynford would be kind enough to allow us bring some of the stalls indoors in the event of rain? Teas would stay out in the stables, of course, and things like hoop-la could carry on on the lawn regardless, so could the plants, but cakes and books and bric-a-brac would be simply ruined."

Heads turned towards Lady Swynford who was feeding a chocolate to her poodle. She pretended, the Colonel saw, to be taken by surprise.

"Goodness, were you asking me something?"

"Whether we could bring some of the stalls inside if it rains, Lady Swynford? Like the year before last."

"I really don't think I could allow it – not after that unfortunate episode." The scarf fluttered.

"The item *was* recovered. And we could get a police constable on duty here to make quite certain nothing like that happens again."

"I couldn't be sure it wouldn't, though, could I?"

Naomi stirred irritably. "It was only an ashtray, for heaven's sake, Ursula. And nothing's ever been pinched before."

"A *silver* ashtray."

"Silver plate, actually. EPNS. And it was just some silly kid who owned up anyway."

"The principle's the same, whatever and whoever it was, Naomi. If I allow the public to come into the house it would mean everything of any value being put away, and there's a very great deal. I'm not sure that I could cope with that in my present state of health."

Mrs Cuthbertson played her only good card. "If it weren't for the urgent need of funds for the church roof, Lady Swynford, I'm sure we none of us would wish to ask it of you. We know what a personal interest you always take, as patron . . ."

The words hung in the air. Lady Swynford appeared to be considering the matter carefully. Everyone waited for her to speak. Naomi, the Colonel saw, looked about to explode.

"Very well. I suppose if they were kept to the hall and the other doors were locked, it would be all right."

"We're very grateful, Lady Swynford." Mrs Cuthbertson seemed to be speaking through gritted teeth.

"So long as nobody uses the downstairs cloakroom. I absolutely refuse to allow that. It was left in a disgusting state last time. That's out of bounds whatever the weather."

"Which brings me to the next item," Mrs Cuthbertson said quickly. "Portaloos."

The discussion over the cost of hiring portable toilets, the number needed and the discreet siting of them occupied the next half hour. It was nearly one o'clock before the meeting dragged to a close and Ruth Swynford rose to pass round glasses of sherry from a decanter on the side. Lady Swynford remained seated, the poodle on her lap, and the Major who was hovering round her, in attendance, beckoned the Colonel over. It was rather like being granted an audience with royalty. She gave him a regal hand and a smile. The poodle on her lap wagged its ridiculous pom-pom tail as though it had never challenged him earlier.

## Old Soldiers Never Die

"We haven't met before, have we? You've bought Pond Cottage, I hear. Charming little place. How are you enjoying living in Frog End?"

"I've only just arrived, so it's hard to answer that yet, Lady Swynford."

"I'm afraid you may find us rather dull, Colonel."

A gallant response was obviously required. "I'm sure I shan't."

"I suppose Major Cuthbertson press-ganged you onto the fête committee? That wasn't very neighbourly of you, Major."

The Major gulped awkwardly at his sherry. "This must seem very mundane after your active army life. Did you serve abroad?"

"Mostly."

"Where was that?"

"Oh, all over the place – where we still have an army."

"How simply fascinating! I'd love to hear all about it. You must come to dinner soon."

Mrs Bentley edged forward for an audience and he finished his sherry quickly and slipped away. In the hall he met Naomi.

"Unspeakable woman, isn't she?" She didn't trouble to specify which woman. "Everybody loathes her, except poor old Roger who's really smitten. Her husband was a jolly decent chap – just the opposite. Really cared about the village. He was engaged to my late sister, years ago, of course. Then along comes Ursula and pinches him from Jess. She was just a chorus girl, or something, you know, but you'd never guess it by the way she acts. I always think the Duchess of Windsor must have been rather the same, more royal than the real royals."

They walked out into the sunshine. He felt deeply depressed by the whole experience of the morning. If it was a taste of his life to come, then he didn't care for it one bit.

53

"Nice old car of yours, Hugh." Naomi admired the Riley. "They don't make 'em like that any more."

"I bought it years ago, in the late fifties. It's been stored in a rented garage most of the time. I liked it too much to get rid of it."

"Good old-fashioned black. You can't beat it." She plonked her huge leather shoulder bag on the fire-engine red bonnet of her Metro and rummaged around in it. "Got a recipe for you, somewhere . . . ah, here it is." She produced a crumpled bit of paper triumphantly and handed it to him. "Simple as falling off a log. It's usually made with leftovers from a roast but I always do it with butcher's mince – not the best, mind, the cheaper stuff has more flavour."

He looked down at the pencilled scrawl.

Sheperd's Pie:
Ingredients: One finly chopped onion
3/4 1b mince
4 flewid ozs beef stock . . .

"You were making a fool of yourself with her, as usual, Roger." Marjorie Cuthbertson crashed the gears of the Escort, turning it in the Manor driveway. "Hanging round her all the time. She just thinks you're a silly old duffer, you know. And the way she treats us all like the local tenantry sticks in my craw."

The car leapt forward sending up spurts of gravel and the Major clutched at the passenger arm rest. He wondered vaguely what a craw was and if Marjorie had even got one. If she had, it was a long time since he'd seen it. It was one of those damned stupid sayings that people used without knowing what they really meant. Like getting one's goat. What on earth could be the origin of that? She was just

## Old Soldiers Never Die

jealous, of course. The green-eyed monster was rearing its head. Now, there was another curious one. Why green? Why not blue? No, that was for being down in the dumps, which was what he often was. You had the blues. And you saw red when you were angry, and had a yellow streak if you were a coward and were browned-off if you were fed up. If you weren't careful you could end up like a damned rainbow.

Anyway, a man could always tell when a woman was interested and Ursula, in his mind he addressed her by her Christian name, had given him some pretty hot looks on the side. Thank God he'd kept his hair, unlike most chaps of his age, and his shape, too. More or less. He patted his stomach surreptitiously under his blazer, bit of a gut there, but not too bad. He really must try and cut down on the booze: that's what did the damage. Maybe press-ups would help? He used to be able to do thirty straight off in the army, but that was a hell of a long time ago.

They shot out of the Manor entrance, narrowly missing the gatepost and the Escort bucked along the road by the village green, swerving in a wide arc to avoid Phillipa Rankin on her bike. Jesus, Marjorie was a terrible driver! Trouble was she'd never had to drive abroad, so she'd only learnt when they came back to England. God knows how she'd ever passed the test – the examiner must have been in shock. Still, only six months till he got his licence back and he was damned if he was going to be driven by her any more then.

He decided to ignore Marjorie's jibe completely. That was the best way to deal with it. Dignified restraint. "As a matter of fact, she's asked us to dinner the week after next. On Friday."

"And I suppose you said yes."

"Difficult to refuse. Not as though we'd be doing much else. She's asking the Colonel, too."

"She'll be getting her claws into him next, wait and see." The Major frowned. The Colonel wasn't a bad-looking chap, he supposed. Quite attractive to some women, probably. And he'd kept his hair, too. Taller than himself, unfortunately, and a bit younger – not that that counted these days. Ursula herself must be in her sixties, though, by God, she didn't look it. The fellow had higher rank, of course, though not by much. A widower, though, and females always felt sorry for *them*, so he'd noticed. Only the rumour was that the Colonel was still pretty cut up about losing his wife, even after a long time, so he wasn't likely to be up for grabs, so to speak. The Major's face cleared and he began to wonder how he'd feel if old Marjorie were to drop off the branch. Not sure he'd carry a torch for the old girl like that. Damned odd to be fancy free again, after all these years. How many was it? Forty? Probably more. He was always forgetting their anniversary. A bloody lifetime . . .

"What a ludicrous old bore the Major is," Lady Swynford said. "I'll really have to speak to him soon if he doesn't stop pestering me."

When the committee members had all left she had moved to the sofa with an exaggerated sigh of relief. Ruth poured her another sherry.

"You encourage him, Mama, you know you do."

"I do nothing of the kind. I'm simply try to be kind, as one would be to a pet dog that follows one around. Like I am to Shoo-Shoo."

"It's not kind to keep feeding him those chocolates. They're bad for him. And it's not kind to Major Cuthbertson to encourage him."

"Poor man. I feel sorry for him, married to an ugly creature like her. She bullies him appallingly, you know."

## Old Soldiers Never Die

"And you tease him appallingly."

"Heavens, Ruth, you're becoming quite sharp and shrewish. It's very unfeminine. I'm not altogether surprised that you haven't married yet if that's the way you speak to men."

Ruth thought: it's the way I should have spoken to Ralph long ago, instead of letting myself be used for years. People treat you the way you're willing to be treated. What we make of our lives is up to us, in the end. 'The fault, dear Brutus, is not in our stars, but in ourselves'.

Her mother sipped at her sherry. "Anyway, I've asked them to dinner the week after next. I feel I can manage to start entertaining again – just a few people. Not that there's much choice round here, but at least the Cuthbertsons know which knife and fork to use. And I suppose I'd better ask Dr Harvey. One always does, once a year. Though I have to say that I much preferred old Dr Wilson. He had a far better bedside manner. Young doctors don't seem to understand how important that is. Dr Harvey is positively *brusque* with me. It's his background, I suppose. They seem to come from anywhere these days."

"I don't expect he's got time to stand around making polite conversation, Mama, he's got lots of other patients to see."

"Dr Wilson *always* made time for his private patients. I wish he hadn't retired. I don't have the same confidence in Dr Harvey. I'm not at all certain he's prescribing the right pills. They seem to make me feel worse, if anything."

"I'm sure he knows what he's doing. He must treat strokes all the time."

Her mother shrugged delicately. "Well, I'll invite him. In which case, I suppose I may as well get the Vicar over with too, at the same time. Kill two birds with one stone. He'll bore us to death, of course, and it's all so complicated with that wife of his in a wheelchair . . . I thought of asking the Colonel.

"An attractive man, didn't you think? I imagined he'd be some dreary old army type, like the Major."

"He seemed very nice. Rather sad, though. I noticed him during the meeting. He was miles away at times."

"I don't blame him. I wish I had been too. Like myself, he must have found it tedious beyond belief."

"Naomi says his late wife was lovely. She saw a photo of her. She thinks he still grieves for her."

"Oh, men always get over losing their wives in the end. It's astonishing the rapid recovery they can sometimes make – in no time at all."

Did that apply to an affair as well as bereavement, Ruth wondered? Did Ralph ever think about her at all now? Probably only with relief that he had ended it. But she still thought about *him*. Constantly.

Phillipa Rankin was pedalling along furiously, head bent. Hell's bells, she was going to be late for her pupil if she didn't get a move on. The blasted meeting had gone on so long, and there'd been no chance for a private word with Lady Swynford, as she'd hoped. Not that she thought it would do much good. The woman was an unfeeling, greedy bitch. If Sir Alan had still been alive she would never have been faced with this nightmare. Or if that stroke had only been fatal. It would have been Ruth in charge now and Ruth was quite different from her mother. She'd taught Ruth to ride and she knew. She was decent like her father.

She turned off the green, sped round the bend and through the water splash, scattering ducks and ducklings, and then turned down the narrow lane that led to her stables. When she had first rented the paddocks from Sir Alan all those years ago it had seemed as though the arrangement would go on as long as she did. He'd always said as much. She'd put up the

## Old Soldiers Never Die

stabling and set about building up her business: teaching young children to ride properly, not just hack around as they did at most riding stables. She'd had pupils who had gone on later to do showjumping and dressage and even one who had ridden with the British Olympic team. The first lessons were vital, in her view. Bad habits learnt at the outset were hard to correct; good ones were ingrained for ever. She'd made a pretty good success of it, though she said it herself and only to herself because there was nobody else really to say it to. She was a one-man band, doing all the work on her own. That was the way she liked it and anyway she couldn't afford to pay for help. For some time now she'd been giving free lessons to disabled pupils as well, because she saw it as doing her bit for a worthwhile cause. But feed prices and everything had gone up and up, and the vet's bills were always astronomical, and she still had the mortgage to pay off on the cottage. The recession hadn't helped one bit: people had stopped sending her pupils because they couldn't afford it. Then Dolly had gone lame and Hector had got too old to work much, which left only Petal and Storm.

And then the solicitor's letter had arrived, like a bolt from the blue. Mr Proudfoot regretted that he had received instructions that the rent was to be increased when her lease came up for renewal next month. Nearly *doubled*, in fact. No prizes for guessing whose idea that had been.

Miss Rankin swooped into the stable yard where her small pupil was waiting with her mother beside a brand new Range Rover. The mother was looking annoyed.

"Frightfully sorry, to keep you. Got held up . . ."

She saddled up her Shetland, Petal, with quick, expert hands and led her out. The child was a complete beginner so they wouldn't do anything other than walk quietly round the paddock, to build her confidence gradually. The trick was never to hurry it. Let her hang on to Petal's mane if she wanted. Just get used to the feeling of being on a horse. She gave her an encouraging smile.

As she led the pony round the paddock, she went on worrying. She'd done the sums over and over again and the answer was always the same. The new rent was more than she could possibly manage so she was going to have to close down the riding school – unless she could somehow persuade Lady Swynford to change her mind. And there was a fat chance of that.

By the end of the hour her pupil had let go of Petal's mane and was holding the reins in both hands and beginning to sit quite well in the saddle. That was the reward, seeing them make progress. Hell's teeth, it was her whole life – the the only thing she cared about. She'd jolly well *got* to find a way.

That evening the Colonel dug out his Gilbert and Sullivan records. He'd collected them since his school days and knew almost every word of every song. He poured himself a whisky and sat down in the wing chair, turning the volume up high to banish the silence and letting the familiar music work its familiar magic.

He beat time with his fingers on the arm of the chair.

> When I was a lad I served a term
> As office boy to an Attorney's firm.
> I cleaned the windows and I swept the floor,
> And I polished up the handle of the big front door.
> I polished up that handle so carefullee
> That now I am the Ruler of the Queen's Navee!

The telephone rang and he rose to answer it, turning down the volume on his way.

## Old Soldiers Never Die

"Dad? How are you getting on?"
It was never anything less than a pleasure to hear Alison's voice.
"Fine. Fine."
"I thought I'd come down this weekend – give you a hand with unpacking things, if that's OK? I could get there by Saturday lunchtime."
His spirits lifted but he had resolved never to become a bloody burden to his children. "I'm getting straight and you must have better things to do."
"No I haven't. And I'd like to see you."
"My next-door neighbour has just given me a recipe for shepherd's pie. Maybe I'll try it out on you at the weekend."
She laughed. "Good idea. See you on Saturday, then."
"I'll look forward to it."
He went back to his whisky and his Gilbert and Sullivan. Saturday was only the day after tomorrow. Not long.

# Five

Alison arrived at midday. The Colonel had been looking out for her at the sitting-room window and saw her Golf drive up and stop outside the front gate. He watched her get out, smart and sophisticated in London clothes. Last time she had seen the cottage the builders had still been in, knocking things about. The transformation impressed her as much as it had impressed Naomi.

"It looks lovely, Dad! Really nice. I must admit I thought you might have made a bit of a mistake, but I was wrong. Mum would have approved."

She often spoke of her mother and he was grateful for it.

"She'd have made a much better job, though." He waved a hand round the sitting-room.

"I think you've done brilliantly. I like it. Nice and plain. No frills."

Her own London flat was plain to the point of starkness: dead white walls, venetian blinds, little furniture and a couple of very modern paintings.

"Where did you get this ratty old thing?" She stroked Thursday who was curled up on the sofa."

"I didn't get him anywhere. He just walked in. It used to be his home."

"Still is, by the look of it. He must be company."

"Not exactly. He generally ignores me, except when he wants to be fed. I'd get rid of him if I had any sense."

"I remember Marcus and I used to wish we could have a cat or dog but, of course, it was hopeless with you and Mum being shunted about abroad and us at boarding school."

They'd never had a proper home, he thought with regret staying in turn with their grandparents for half-terms and being flown out for the holidays to whichever army quarters he and Laura happened to be occupying at the time. The only real continuity had been school.

Alison was taking off her jacket. "Well, I'll help you get the rest of those boxes unpacked."

"Later. First we'll go and get some lunch at the Dog and Duck."

"What no shepherd's pie?"

"I've decided we're eating out this weekend."

Over their steak and kidney pies in the pub, she said, "I'm glad to hear your're trying to do some proper cooking. You've been living out of tins and on those gruesome telly suppers for far too long. Awfully bad for you."

"You sound just like my neighbour."

"The one who gave you the recipe? What's she like?"

"Very friendly. Very frank. Very nice."

"Spinster?"

"No. She's a widowed divorcee."

"Watch out, she's probably after you."

He laughed. "You haven't met her, or you'd know she isn't."

She gave him her direct look. "Seriously, Dad, I hope you do find someone some day . . . I'd be happy for you. So would Marcus. I want you to know that."

He smiled at her. "I don't think I could ever replace your mother, Alison, but thank you. How about *you* finding someone, as you put it? I'd be happy for you, too, if you did that."

## Old Soldiers Never Die

She made a face. "I've never met anyone I'd want to spend the rest of my life with. Or anyone who'd want to spend his with me. You and Mum were so lucky like that. Perfect for each other."

"Yes, we were very lucky."

He'd often told himself so. Many times. They'd had nearly thirty wonderful years and most people weren't that fortunate. Nothing could take that away.

"Besides," Alison went on lightly, "I love my job and I earn good money. I'm not sure I need a man. He'd expect me to iron his shirts and I hate ironing."

"Find one who doesn't expect it."

"Easier said than done."

They smiled at each other. I hope she finds him, though, he thought. Somewhere and soon.

On Sunday they went to church. It had been Alison's idea. "I want to see what the locals are like." For her sake he was happy to go through the motions, and he'd always enjoyed singing the hymns.

The church was fuller than he had expected when so many were near empty. There was a good deal of covert curiosity directed their way and he realised, with amusement, that it was mainly at Alison. They all knew about him by now, but not about her. He could see them wondering who, and what, she was and in her black linen jacket and trousers, long hair tied back with a coloured scarf, she didn't look particularly daughterly. The Major's eyes were popping out on stalks.

Few of the women bothered with hats these days, he noticed. Even the older ones, though Mrs Cuthbertson sported a shapeless felt and Miss Butler a neat navy straw, and Mrs Fox of teas was wearing some kind of beret. He spotted Naomi's bare grey thatch towards the front.

## Margaret Mayhew

Lady Swynford made her entrance last of all – like the mother of the bride – heels tapping down the nave, leaning on her daughter's arm. She wore not only a hat, an expensive-looking creation with a veil, but gloves too. They took their seats alone in the front pew.

The choir shuffled in, followed by the Vicar, the organ wheezed suddenly from its corner and the first hymn began.

> He who would valiant be,
> Gainst all disaster,
> Let him in constancy
> Follow the Master.
> There's no discouragement
> Shall make him once relent
> His first avowed intent
> To be a pilgrim.

They droned on sounding anything but valiant. The organist, whoever it was, seemed to be playing slower and slower. The Colonel knew the words by heart and his attention wandered. It was a lovely old church. The barrel-vaulted roof looked around fifteenth century to him, with some interesting carving: winged angels, a grinning devil's head, a sun, animals, even what looked like a monkey. The windows were of the same period, he thought, though their stained glass, like the pews, was clearly Victorian.

England's churches, he mused, looking up at the beautiful roof again, were one of her great glories, and each one of them a testament to several hundred of years of parish history. It was all there: the names of every priest; the local families; the coats of arms; the tombs and tributes; monuments and memorials; the lists of the war dead . . .

He let his mind drift on through the lessons, the prayers, the

## Old Soldiers Never Die

Te Deum (which he thought was going to grind to a complete stop), the Jubilate (mercifully shorter and quicker) the parish notices (marriage banns, the Mother's Union coffee morning, a bible study group meeting at the Vicarage, a churchwardens' meeting. They stood for another hymn, 'Take up thy cross, the Saviour said', and then sat down again for the sermon. The Vicar had taken moral and spiritual courage as his theme and he went on about it at some length. The Colonel sensed the congregation's restlessness around him; there were coughs and throat-clearings and creakings from the pews. The Major looked at his watch, held it to his ear and shook it.

The Colonel made a point of grasping the Vicar's hand very firmly as they left the church. "Excellent sermon."

"Thank you, Colonel." The Vicar's face lit up.

He wondered if anyone else in his flock ever told him that.

Naomi came striding up. "Good to see you, Hugh." She was actually wearing a skirt and ordinary shoes.

"This is my daughter, Alison."

He introduced her to the few people he had met and observed their surprise in some cases and, in the Major's, frank disbelief almost to the point of digging him in the ribs. Perhaps retired Colonels weren't supposed to have glamorously attractive daughters.

Alison left soon after teatime to drive back to London. It was the moment he had privately dreaded when he would have to face the silence again. He wandered from room to room, not knowing what to do. There was nothing he wanted to watch on television or to listen to on the radio. It was too early for a drink but it would pass the time to make a cup of tea. He went into the kitchen and filled the kettle. While waiting for it to boil he looked out of the kitchen window and saw someone in the jungle. A man was standing among the brambles, looking about. The Colonel opened the back door.

"Can I help?"

Bloody silly question, he thought. I should be asking what the hell he's doing there. He looks damned odd. A bit loopy. For a moment he thought the man was going to make off, but he seemed to think better of it and stood his ground. He took off his canvas hat and stood clutching it against to his chest.

Light dawned. It would be the gardener from the Manor that Naomi had spoken of. He must have got in round the side by the garage. Probably too nervous to come to the front door. Definitely a bit odd. The Colonel went out, advancing casually and with a friendly smile. "Come to give me a hand with clearing all this?"

A jerky nod in answer.

"I'd certainly appreciate it. I'll never manage it by myself."

Another nod.

"Could you start soon?"

He mumbled something that sounded like, " 'Morrow evenin'." and turned tail suddenly, loping away through the nettle patch by the privy, apparently unharmed by them. The Colonel shook his head and went back into the cottage to make his tea.

That night he woke up around three, as he often did. Almost every night, in fact. Sometimes, as in this case, it was when he had been dreaming about Laura – always a vivid dream in which she was so alive and real that when he awoke he stretched out his hand to feel for her beside him. The space was empty and cold. The realisation brutal.

After that he didn't sleep at all. He seldom did once he had started to think about her – to remember the two long years of suffering he had watched her endure. The out-patient hospital visits, the long waits for the treatment that she had undergone without complaint. Then the stays in hospital, with periods in

## Old Soldiers Never Die

between at home that had given them false hope. Then a longer stay that had turned into a permanency. He thought of the ward and its spurious atmosphere of optimism; of hope where there was none. The Big Conspiracy. The jolly game that everyone in it played. Jokey cards, bright flowers, the nurses' well-meant but relentless bullying, 'Come along now, Laura, let's get you sitting up today'. He could see himself walking the length of that ward, with dread in his heart and yet another bunch flowers in his hand, and he could see Laura's face on the pillow, trying to smile up at him. Her hair had started to grow back – a faint, dark stubble on her skull – so that, with her sunken cheeks, her hollow eyes and her emaciated arms she had looked exactly like a Belsen inmate. There had been times when he had almost broken down in front of her, but somehow he had kept going. Kept visiting. Kept smiling. He had almost no recollection of how he had got through the hours back in the rented London flat, except that he had drunk a lot of whisky and done a lot of staring out of the window. Once, on the way back from the hospital, he had found himself going into a church, a dark and gloomy sort of place he remembered, full of grimy stone and ugly Victorian stained glass.

He had always been a Christmas and Easter sort of man – singing the hymns loudly, rattling through the Creed and saying amen in the right places – but this time he had sunk to his knees and prayed to God to spare Laura; to make her miraculously well again; to give her back, not to take her away. A priest had passed him and he had realised that the place was Catholic. On the way out he had bought a candle and lit it, without knowing exactly why or for what. He had watched the flame flicker unsteadily in a draught and burn as faintly and precariously as Laura's life.

And in the end, she had died alone in a hospital room. He

had not been there with her because it had happened in the middle of the night, quite suddenly. Not even a nurse had been at her side. At the end, he had failed her and left her to go alone.

He went through it all over again, unable to stop torturing himself. After a while he heard a cockerel start to crow and the birds begin to twitter in the eaves outside the bedroom window. He lay there, watching and waiting for the dawn.

The Vicar was awake, too. During the daytime he could convince himself that he was doing a good job in the parish, but at night the demons of self-doubt came out to plague him. His sermon had fallen as flat as all the others, though the Colonel had been kind enough to have a word of praise. The rest of them had long since given up the pretence. Lady Swynford had been even more cutting than usual, "I couldn't follow it at all, Vicar. Quite beyond me." And yet he had felt inspired in the writing of it. Felt that he was saying something they would all understand: that moral and spiritual courage was far harder to find and sustain than the physical counterpart, and far more potent. It could endure all things, accomplish all things, overcome all things. He lacked it, of course, himself. He was afraid all the time: of Lady Swynford, of the Bishop, of dismal failure in his ministry, even, sometimes, of losing his own faith.

Jean stirred beside him and he listened for a while to her regular breathing. As always, asleep, or awake, she comforted him.

Freda Butler heard the cockerel crowing. She had been awake for what seemed like hours, and had got up to go to the bathroom three times. It was getting worse and becoming quite a problem. She'd had to excuse herself in the middle of

## Old Soldiers Never Die

the last Guides' meeting and some of the girls had sniggered. She would *have* to go and see the doctor about it, however much she dreaded the thought of discussing anything so personal. Dr Wilson wouldn't have been so bad, but Dr Harvey was so *young* – young enough to be her son . . . if she'd ever had one. It was going to take all her courage to go to the surgery and find the words to explain. She lay there, worrying about it for a while, and knowing that if she didn't fall asleep soon, she'd have to get up and go along the passage yet again.

She tried to let her mind go blank but, instead, found herself thinking about Lady Swynford, which always upset her. The way she had behaved at the fête committee meeting had been typical, queening it over everyone, putting on that oh-so-gracious act and then making petty difficulties. And the way she'd summoned people over to talk to her at the end, *just* as though she were royalty when really she was nothing special at all. Freda had looked her up in *Burke's Peerage and Baronetage* in the library: Ursula Gladys, only daughter of Norman and Elsie Hobbs. That didn't sound anything to be so superior about. And there'd been a rumour in the village that she'd been some kind of dancer before she'd ensnared Sir Alan, though of course that might not be true. One had to be fair. Well, try to be. What certainly *was* true was that she'd taken him away from Mrs Grimshaw's poor sister; but that wouldn't have worried a woman like Lady Swynford. Not a jot.

Miss Butler turned over in bed and pummelled hard at the pillow. Naturally she herself hadn't been summoned to the presence. Being an admiral's daughter apparently counted for nothing. Lady Swynford always treated her as though she simply didn't exist, which was more insulting than being snubbed. Whenever their paths actually crossed, like outside the church that morning, she looked straight through her, as though she were completely invisible. Miss Butler closed her eyes and imagined a scene in which she had suddenly, somehow, become both very rich and very famous. Lady Swynford was coming up to her, all eager smiles, and she turned away, cutting her dead . . .

Feeling better, she slept.

# Six

"Aquilegia," Naomi said. "Or columbine to you, I expect. Seeds itself all over the place."

The Colonel admired the delicate pink flowers just coming into bloom all around the terrace at the back of Pear Tree Cottage. "They aren't anything to me. I can't tell a daffodil from a daisy."

"You'll soon learn. Have to, if you want to get that garden of yours into shape. How's Jacob doing?"

"Performing miracles. He's cleared a lot of it already. There *is* a pond there, by the way, in one corner. It's badly silted up, but it's there. Complete with frogspawn. I thought I'd have a go at dredging it out. I rather like the idea of having frogs in Frog End."

"Handy to have them around. They'll eat a lot of pests for you."

They progressed slowly round Naomi's garden, followed by her two Jack Russels, Mutt and Jeff, who were a great improvement on Shoo-Shoo. He wondered if his own garden, next door, would ever approach the charm and natural beauty of this place where everything seemed to be growing as though it had planted itself.

"A lot of it has," Naomi said, when he remarked on this. "I like it that way. Plants know what's good for them and you can't make one grow properly where it doesn't want to. The self-sown ones'll find exactly the right places for themselves and look right there, too. Let nature take its course is my maxim – though she's gone much too far in your case, of course."

He bent his head as they walked under the blossoming pear tree and down the side of a border. Naomi pointed out the budding plants as they went along.

"Dianthus, artemesia, white valerian, lavender – all sun lovers. Meconopsis, lupins – a mixed bag there – echinopsis at the back, the thistle family. Now *they*'ll take over if I let them, but they're nice old things and useful for flower arrangements. Alchemilla, Welsh poppies, delphiniums – all blues, I don't like the pinks. They're a lot of work with the staking, but worth it . . ." her hand swept across the border ". . . all this lot will be in their glory next month."

They strolled on towards the end of the garden where a mass of beautiful spring flowers grew in the rough grass by the stone wall.

The Colonel smiled. "I know what those are, at least," he said. "They're bluebells."

There was a lean-to greenhouse in the corner against the wall and she showed him the trays of young plants on the slatted shelves. "Annuals for the fête plant stall. Petunias, mostly. Can't stand the things myself but they always sell well. I propagate most of my own stuff, can't afford garden-centre prices. Don't care for the places, anyway. They've usually bought in and the plants are half dead."

As they walked back towards the cottage he asked her if she would help him choose plants for his garden.

"I'll help you not to make too many mistakes," she said. "And I'll lend you one of my gardening books, but you must do the choosing yourself or it won't be *your* garden. That's the point of it all, see?"

## Old Soldiers Never Die

He wasn't sure if he did see. As long as the thing got done, it didn't seem to him to matter how.

"Have you tried the shepherd's pie yet?"

"I made a stab at it." He'd gone into Dorchester to buy the mince and onions and potatoes. The onions had burnt, the mince gone into hard little grey granules, and the mashed potatoes were full of lumps. He had eaten a few mouthfuls and then given the rest to Thursday who had sniffed at it and walked away.

"It takes practice," she said cheerfully. "You'll do better next time. What else are you eating?"

"Oh, eggs and things . . . I can boil them and scramble them and poach them. And I bake potatoes in the microwave oven."

"Get yourself a simple cook book," she recommended. "You know the sort of thing: *Easy Cooking for One.*"

It sounded infinitely depressing, but he didn't say so.

"Sit down, Colonel. What can I do for you?"

Dr Harvey was far younger than he had expected – not more than in his thirties, which was momentarily disconcerting. He'd have preferred to talk to an older man and was already regretting the whole idea.

"I haven't been sleeping too well. Could you give me something to help?" Embarrassment made him sound curt.

"How long haven't you been sleeping well?"

He couldn't remember exactly; it seemed for ever – since Laura had become ill and he had known he was going to lose her. "Quite a while. It varies. Lately it's been bad for some reason."

"You're widower." It was a statement, not a question.

"My wife died ten years ago, yes."

The doctor gave him a sympathetic look. "Widowers often

find it a lot tougher to cope than widows, in my experience. Even after several years."

One always forgot that doctors had seen and heard it all before, hundreds of times: human fraility at its lowest ebb – grief, pain, fear, loneliness.

"I've adjusted reasonably well, I hope."

"I'm sure you have, Colonel. What I'm not so sure is whether the pills will help much. And they can be addictive."

"Does that matter, at my age?"

"It does in my book. You've got years of useful life ahead of you. Sixty-five is nothing these days. I'll give you a prescription for a few. After that you're on your own."

I'm on my own already, he thought drily. He took the piece of paper and left the surgery. Useful for *what* exactly?

Jacob was getting on like a house on fire, cutting great swathes through the jungle. The Colonel watched him at work from the kitchen window. The garden had been cleared almost down to the wall at the far end, and the long flower bed that Naomi had probed with her stick had emerged. He still had no idea what was growing in it, or which were weeds and which were plants and he would have to ask her. She had lent him a gardening book, complete with colour photographs, and he had started to read it in the evenings.

He had tried to give Jacob a hand, but he obviously preferred to be left alone to get on with it. An odd customer, if ever there was one. Never looked you straight in the eye and mumbled away in his Dorset accent so that you could scarcely understand a word of it. When he'd asked Jacob what he owed him he'd either had no idea, or wouldn't say. So, he'd have to ask Naomi about that, too. God, he'd become a perfect nuisance to her, if he wasn't careful.

## Old Soldiers Never Die

Someone was knocking at the front door and he went to answer it. The Vicar stood there, looking apologetic.

"Probably an inconvenient time for you, Colonel, but I was passing and thought I'd take a chance . . ."

"Not at all. Please come in."

He showed him into the sitting-room. The poor chap obviously felt guilty about not calling before, so they might as well get it over with.

"What can I offer you? Whisky?"

He saw a look of gratitude replace the one of apology.

"Thank you so much, Colonel. That would be very kind."

He fetched the glasses and ice from the kitchen and returned to find him still standing awkwardly in the middle of the room.

"Do sit down, Vicar. Ice? Water? Soda?"

"Just some soda would be very nice, thank you."

The man looked exhausted and in need of a stiff one. The Colonel poured a good tot and squirted in a splash of soda. The Vicar took it with a wry smile.

"I'm usually given sherry."

"Not much of a pick-me-up after a hard day's work."

"It's been a busy one," the Vicar admitted. "But then it nearly always is. So much to do with three parishes to cover."

"Your good health."

"Oh, and yours, Colonel." He took a gulp of the whisky and colour came into his cheeks. "Quite strong . . ."

"It'll do you good."

"Yes, perhaps it will. I'm sorry not to have called sooner – not because of the whisky, of course. I hope you're settling down well in Frog End."

"I'm making progress. Frankly, it's not easy getting used to being retired. Passing one's sell-by date, as they put it in shops."

77

"God will find a way for you to go forward."

Politeness prevented him from replying that he had lost any faith in God. Laura's suffering had killed off any lingering expectations in that direction. He wondered how on earth with all the cruel and unjust human misery and misfortune that they must encounter priests ever managed to sustain theirs.

"Beautiful old church you have, Vicar," he said instead, leading the conversation onto safer ground. "Around fifteenth century, I thought?"

"Oh, yes, indeed. And parts of it even earlier: the tower dates from the mid-thirteenth. You may have noticed the Early English lancet windows. And we have a number of other very interesting features. Did you happen to see the Swynford monument in the north chapel?"

"Not yet."

"It's worth close inspection. It dates from the early part of the seventeenth century and is particularly fine."

"The Swynford family have been here a long while, then?"

The Vicar nodded. "Since the late fifteenth century. And they have held the patronage for more than a hundred and fifty years. I was appointed by Sir Alan a few years before he died."

The Colonel was curious. "What happened then?"

"The patronage passed to Lady Swynford."

God help the poor chap, he thought. "I didn't know that sort of thing existed these days."

"Oh yes, there are still private patrons. I shall always be grateful to Sir Alan for the chance he gave me. Of course," the Vicar continued delicately, as though the Colonel had read his thoughts, "the living is in my possession until I reach the age of seventy – a good many years hence, I'm glad to say. Except in exceptional circumstances."

The Colonel wondered what those would be. Flagrant

## Old Soldiers Never Die

adultery with a parishioner? Abuse of trust and position, like a doctor with a patient? From what he'd seen of both the Vicar and the local ladies such a thing was highly unlikely. The man was quite safe.

"It's certainly a very pleasant spot. There must be many parishes that are not quite so idyllic."

"Indeed there are. I was a curate in Bermondsey for quite some time and then incumbent of a parish in the East End – that's where I met my wife, in fact. She was helping in a Youth Centre there. I came very late to the ministry, you see. I was a teacher for a number of years before I realised that that was what I wanted to do with my life. I didn't take holy orders until I was nearly forty."

The Colonel smiled. "The Church obviously treats its recruits rather better than the army. At that age the army would consider you almost over the hill. They retire most of us at fifty-five."

The Vicar hesitated. "When you've settled in we'd always be glad of any time you might have to spare – reading the lesson, cutting the grass . . ."

"I'll certainly bear that in mind."

"I don't suppose you're a bell-ringer by any chance. I know they're looking for someone?"

"I'm afraid not. May be I'll learn one day. When I've sorted myself out."

"Yes, indeed . . . you must take your time."

"The other half, Vicar?"

"Goodness me, no thank you. I really must be on my way. I have a choir practice. Thank you for the drink."

The Colonel saw him out with relief. He was a decent, sincere sort of chap, who meant well, but he was thankful to be rid of him.

\* \* \*

*Margaret Mayhew*

Miss Hartshorne had already begun the practice when he got there and the choir were halfway through 'Thy hand, O God, has guided'. She stopped playing the organ as he hurried down the nave; the singing petered out raggedly.
"We thought we'd better make a start, Vicar."
"Yes, of course. I'm sorry, I'm a bit late."
Ten minutes late, which would never do. The children had school homework and suppers to get back to, and the three adult members would be fretting about missing some TV programme. He took his place, hoping that none of them could smell whisky on his breath. Notionally, Miss Hartshorne was in charge, but he had found that she couldn't keep order among the children, especially the boys. His presence was required to put a stop to the whispering and giggling and dart-throwing, at least, as best he could. Sometimes it was hopeless. There seemed to be no discipline these days. Parents didn't think it important, or enforce it, so it was no use complaining to them. And anyway it was hard enough to get any children to join the choir at all. Most of them only did so for a short period, and he had heard all excuses imaginable for not attending the practices. He looked at the two empty places.
"Where's Tommy this evening?"
Tommy's sister went red. "He's not feeling well. He's got a bad cold."
He knew by the blush that it wasn't true. "And Peter? Does anyone know what's happened to him?" Nobody did, of course, or if they did, they weren't saying. He sighed. There were few enough of them already. "Well, we'd better start from the beginning again. Miss Hartshorne?"

Thy hand, O God, has guided
Thy flock, from age to age;

## Old Soldiers Never Die

> The wondrous tale is written,
> Full clear, on every page . . .

The singing was really poor. They weren't even properly together and nobody seemed to be making the slightest effort. He held up his hand.

"Miss Hartshorne . . . I'm sorry, but would you mind? I really think we ought to be able to do better than this. It's a beautiful hymn and we should be singing the words as though we all meant them – what's the matter, Kevin?"

"Nothing."

"Then please stop making those silly faces. Now, let's try again, and put some feeling into it. And keep together."

They started off once more, slightly better, and he beat time firmly with his hand. None of them really cared, of course, and not one had a decent voice, except for Matthew. He sang like an angel and looked like one too, with his fair hair and blue eyes. The Vicar watched the boy as they sang on through the next verse, soothed by the sound of his voice, pure and true above the rest. It was a thousand pities that his mother wouldn't hear of him trying for a choir school. He'd tried his best but got nowhere with her.

> Our fathers own'd Thy goodness,
> And we their deeds records;
> And both of this bear witness,
> One Church, one Faith, one Lord.

They practised two more hyms and the responses which had been terrible lately. The congregation scarcely attempted them and left it up to the choir. Last Sunday he had been singing almost on his own.

He kept them late and they were all out of the church like

greyhounds out of a trap. Even Miss Hartshorne scuttled off before he could have a word with her. There was probably something special on television that she didn't want to miss. He went to turn off the chancel lights and then saw that Matthew had lingered in the nave.

"Can I have a word with you, please, sir?" He was the only one of them who called him 'sir'.

"Of course, Matthew." He put a kindly hand on the boy's shoulder.

"It's about choir school . . . do you think you could ask my mum about that, again, sir? I'd like to have a go at it, if I can. I really enjoy singing and I think I'm quite good at it."

"You're *very* good at it, Matthew. But I don't think your mother is very keen on the idea."

"Could you speak to her about it again, sir?"

He hesitated, he didn't think Matthew's mother would ever change her mind. It was what was known these days as a one-parent family and he had several like it in his parishes. There was no father around and she must have been very young when Matthew was born, perhaps only sixteen, or so; her son was all she had.

The boy was looking up at him pleadingly. "Please, sir."

"All right, I'll try once more."

"Now, sir?" Against his better judgement he drove the boy back to his home in the cul-de-sac of council houses at the edge of the village. His mother must have been looking out of her front window because she flung open the door and came running down the path.

"What happened? Why is he so late?" She clutched at Matthew, pulling him to her. "What have you been doing with him? I've been ever so worried." Her accusing eyes were exactly the same blue as her son but her hair was the colour and texture of old straw. Matthew wriggled free and slipped away into the house.

"I'm so sorry, Mrs Davis." He always called her that out of politeness, though he doubted she had ever been married. "Choir practice went on rather long – I thought I'd give him a lift home."

"I'm not letting him come no more if this goes on."

He knew it was hopeless but he'd promised the boy. "That would be such a pity, Mrs Davis. Matthew has a beautiful voice, you know. Quite exceptional. I was wondering if you'd reconsider about him applying for a place at choir school—"

She cut him short. "I've told you before, I don't want him going away. He's not doing it and that's all there is to be said."

Her voice had risen. They were standing out on the macadam pathway and he knew without turning his head that net curtains would be twitching all around them. The whole road would be watching and listening and enjoying the scene.

He made one last effort, for Matthew's sake. "Please, Mrs Davis, think about it, at least. If Matthew was accepted at Salisbury, he wouldn't be very far away. He would still be able to come home regularly and he would have the benefit of the finest schooling – as well as the chance to serve God in a very special way."

"I don't believe in God no more. What's He ever done for me? And I don't want you interfering with Matthew. He's *my* son. You leave him alone!"

Before he could say another word she had turned and rushed back into the house. He was left standing on the path, facing the slammed door. With as much dignity as he could muster he turned and went back to his car knowing that dozens of eyes would be upon him.

# Seven

The pond was choked with weeds and covered with green scum. The Colonel worked away, pulling at the slimy tangle with his bare hands and dumping it into the wheelbarrow. Thursday sat watching him impassively from the bank, front paws placed neatly together.

He edged further out and his wellington boots sank deeper into the muddy bottom; if he wasn't careful the water would go over the top of them. The pond was bigger than he'd realised and was going to be a hell of a lot of work to clear. Maybe he'd get Jacob back onto the job. And then, again, maybe it might be a bit of a challenge to do it himself. He wiped the sweat off his forehead and started on another patch of weed.

"Yoo-hoo! Hugh! Are you around?"

"Over here."

Naomi came round the side of the cottage and advanced across the grass, carrying something in her arms. Mutt and Jeff trotted after her and circled, exploring with their noses to the ground. Thursday held his position, unblinking, and the dogs gave him a respectful berth.

"So there's your pond, Hugh . . . never noticed it before. The garden had already gone to pot by the time Jess and I moved in, so it must have been hidden by all the brambles. Looks like it's going to be quite a job."

He smiled up at her. "Well, Pond Cottage ought to have a pond."

"I agree. I've got a Pear Tree."

"I'm trying not to disturb the frogspawn."

"Very green of you." She looked around. "Jacob's done well. Another transformation. Now it's time for Phase Two. I've brought you a garden-warming present." She held out a potted plant. "*Lavandula spicata*, or good old common lavender. Hidcote variety so it won't grow too tall. I took some cuttings from mine last year."

He climbed out of the pond to take it from her, boots squelching. "How kind of you. Thank you very much. Where do you think it ought to go?"

"Up to you. It'll like sun and some space to grow. You've got plenty of blanks in the border."

"It was full of weeds. Jacob got rid of most of them."

"Good. You'll have to keep at it, though. And get more stuff planted in so it can all get a good start this year. Have you read the book I lent you?"

"I'm halfway through. And I went into Dorchester and bought some tools and a lawnmower. And these boots."

"Jolly good. You'll soon get the hang of it all. Just remember this is chalky soil, though, so don't go buying azaleas or rhododendrons because they'll hate it – gloomy things anyway, in my opinion."

He peered at the plant she had given him. "When will this flower?"

"Around July. Trim it back in late summer. You can dry the flowers, too, but I don't suppose you'll want to bother with all that." She nodded at the cat. "Thursday's still with you, then?"

"Unfortunately."

"I'd take it as a compliment if I were you, Hugh. Cats are *very* choosy. Well, I'm off."

## Old Soldiers Never Die

She strode away without a backward glance, Mutt and Jeff obediently in tow. That was one of the things he liked most about her: she never wasted time dithering.

"It's quite a simple operation, Miss Butler. One or two of my patients with a similar problem to yourself have had it and with excellent results."

Somehow she had managed to put it into words – muddled sort of ones, she knew, but Dr Harvey had seemed to understand straight away. He had saved her the embarrassment of explaining any further by describing her symptoms back to her exactly. And the examination hadn't been as much of an ordeal as she had feared because he had somehow put her at her ease. He really was a very nice young man. She liked his smile and his frank way of talking to her in his north-country accent, and he had given her good news.

"How soon could I have it?"

"Unfortunately there's a rather long waiting list, unless you could afford to go privately?"

"How much would that cost."

"Somewhere in the region of two thousand pounds, with the surgeon's and anaesthetist's fees and hospital care."

"Goodness, I couldn't possibly manage that. Oh dear, how long, do you think I'd have to wait on the National Health?"

"A year. Maybe eighteen months."

"Oh, dear," she said again, quite downcast by the prospect. Another year or more of discomfort and disturbed nights, and of all the awkwardness.

"I'm sorry," he said sympathetically. "I'll do what I can to hurry things along for you, I promise."

"Thank you, Doctor."

She walked back to Lupin Cottage, thoroughly depressed. There was nothing to be done. She dared not touch her savings unless it was absolutely necessary. If only Father had left her a little more instead of bequeathing almost everything to that naval museum. Of course it was nice that they had his picture on the wall, but even so, she had been his daughter. She went inside and into the sitting-room. Her father stared at her indifferently from the top of the bureau. I don't think he could have cared very much, she thought, in fact, I don't think he really cared at all. Tears suddenly came into her eyes and started to trickle slowly down her cheeks.

Ruth Swynford foraged through her dressing-table drawer for a lipstick. There was one somewhere and she'd better make a bit of an effort this evening. Her hands were a mess, as usual – scratched all over from tying back the rose which had come away from the wall – and her nails wouldn't seem to come clean. Still, she'd done the best with them that she could and nobody was going to notice anyway. She found the lipstick at the back of the drawer; it was the wrong colour to go with her dress, but what the hell? She put the lipstick on and brushed her hair quickly and then went down to see how Mrs Hunt was getting along with the dinner – watercress soup, roast leg of lamb with new potatoes and peas, fruit salad and cheese – there was nothing that could go very wrong there. No unfortunate flights of foreign fancy from one of Mrs Hunt's package holidays that had sometimes turned out almost inedible. Mrs Hunt, large bottom in the air, was bent over the Aga, basting the joint, and everything seemed to be under control. As she came out of the kitchen wing into the hall, her mother was descending the stairs in her slinky Jean Muir gown. She wondered if it was for Major Cuthbertson's benefit? Not very likely that Mama would waste any effort on him. It wasn't for Dr Harvey because he was out of favour for being too brusque, and certainly not for the poor old Vicar.

## Old Soldiers Never Die

So, it must be for the Colonel. He was an attractive man, as Mama had predictably observed: tall, upright, and with that thick, silvery hair.

The Cuthbertsons were the first to arrive – the Major sprucely groomed and exuding a powerful blend of whisky and cologne; Mrs Cuthbertson in a long black velvet skirt and a purple polka-dot blouse with a Margaret Thatcher pussy-cat bow. The Colonel arrived soon after, and she watched her mother being her most charming with him. Yes, the effort was definitely for the Colonel, though she was still keeping the Major on a string and giving it a little tug from time to time. When the Vicar and his wife arrived there was some unavoidable commotion with the wheelchair – he, poor man, looking flustered and apologetic while his wife remained perfectly calm.

Ruth liked Jean Beede. Everybody did, except for Mama. She was so cheerful and matter-of-fact about her infirmity. The irony was that *he* quite obviously relied on her, rather than the other way around. Before the illness had taken its toll, she must have been a pretty woman and, in spite of it, she was still good-looking in her own way, especially her eyes which were large and bright. The Colonel, she noticed, was paying more attention to her than to her mother, bending to hear what she was saying and smiling at whatever it was.

Dr Harvey was the last to arrive – very late in fact, which would earn him more black marks from Mama. Ruth could tell, though, that unlike the Vicar, he didn't care. An urgent call, he said, with only the briefest apology. He was placed beside her at dinner, while the Colonel and Major Cuthbertson flanked her mother. Mrs Cuthbertson was next to the Colonel, and the Vicar and Mrs Beede were at the end, in limbo. She had tried to persuade Mama to arrange it differently, but without success. ('I can't possibly have that dreary little man near me, and I've never liked *her*. She's sly.')

Astute would have been a much better word, Ruth thought, catching Jean's eye across the table and seeing her dry amusement at their isolation. She had manoeuvred the wheelchair to the table by herself, and very deftly, so deftly that she gave the impression somehow of being quite normal, as though she could easily get up and walk if she wished. Only the deformed hands, clawed awkwardly round her knife and fork, betrayed how badly the arthritis had affected her.

"You look as though you've been having a fight with a tiger." Dr Harvey nodded at her own scratched forearms and hands.

"Not a tiger, with 'Madame Gregoire Staechelin'. She's very beautiful but she has sharp claws."

"A cat?"

"No, a climbing rose. She fell off the wall and needed help to get back."

"Did you put something on those scratches?"

"No, Doctor."

"They're quite bad."

"I'm always getting scratched; they clear up."

"Even so . . . how long since you had a tetanus jab?"

"Never."

"You should, you know. It's a sensible precaution."

"It's nice of you to be concerned when I'm not even your patient."

"I'm glad about that."

"Oh?"

"Yes. It means I can ask you out to dinner without being struck off."

She laughed politely at the joke. He was a very good doctor, she'd heard, if village opinions were anything to go by and

## Old Soldiers Never Die

they usually were, but she hadn't had a day's illness since leaving London, and couldn't remember when she'd last consulted a doctor herself. Mama held his north-country accent against him, of course, as well as his manner but, personally, she found his bluntness far preferable to the bland reassurances of Dr Wilson which had left her totally unprepared for Papa's death. And she couldn't blame Dr Harvey for his shortness with Mama who expected far more attention and time than most GPs had to give.

"How do you think my mother looks? She seems to be making good progress."

He glanced towards the end of the table where her mother was talking to the Colonel, her hand resting possessively on his sleeve. "Yes, I'd say she is."

"I'm grateful for all your help, Doctor Harvey."

"Tom, please. And I mean it about the dinner."

Oh Lord, she thought in surprise as she encountered his eyes, he really does. Now what? She'd never given him the slightest encouragement, so far as she was aware. The best thing was to treat it as the joke she'd first taken it for. She said lightly, "Then I wouldn't be able to consult you if I needed to, so I'm afraid I'll have to decline."

The Major took yet another gulp of wine. Damn it, he wished Ursula would pay him a bit more attention. She'd been talking to the Colonel non-stop and he could hardly get a word in. What was she playing at? She'd given him that hot look in the drawing-room before dinner, enough to set the old blood moving and everything else too. Just for a second, then, he'd wondered if he was still up to it. But of course he was! He was still a jolly virile chap, even though there wasn't a lot of practice these days. Well, none at all, as a matter of fact. That sort of thing had pretty well fizzled out, and Marjorie had never been keen anyway – not like himself. Now, when he'd been a bachelor he'd got around – yes, indeed. How many was it? Well, quite a few . . . he just couldn't remember them all now.

He took another quick swig and tried to get in on the conversation but Ursula kept her back turned to him. Of course, a woman in her position had to be careful. She wouldn't want anyone to guess about their affair. *Affair!* The very word sent his ticker thumping and he took another swallow to steady himself. Yes, that was it. She was pulling the wool over their eyes. Daft expression that – people didn't usually go about putting wool on people's heads. Putting up a smokescreen, then. That was better. Damned clever of her. Nobody would guess she cared two hoots for him

He felt something touch his foot and his hopes rose. By Jove, she was playing footsie! He moved his own foot playfully. No, she wasn't, it was just that confounded poodle sniffing at his ankle. He aimed a quick kick and missed.

Yes, that's what she was up to: covering her tracks. Just the same, he wished she'd stop talking to the bloody Colonel and say something to him.

What a silly old fool Roger was, Marjorie Cuthbertson thought dispassionately. She could read him like a book. He was still fancying his chances with Lady Swynford, imagining all sorts of stupid things. Couldn't he see that she was just playing with him, like a cat with a mouse? Teasing him. Making fun of him, poor old Roger. And she'd end up hurting him badly – not that she'd care about that. Ursula Swynford was a cruel woman and she, for one, disliked her intensely. More than that, she actually *hated* her. Who did she think she was, anyway? No decent background, in spite of all those airs and graces, anyone who actually had one could tell that. She'd

## Old Soldiers Never Die

been on the stage once, or something, so rumour had it, and everyone knew what *those* sort of people got up to. If it wasn't for the sake of the church roof she herself wouldn't be sitting here, putting up with it all. One had to make sacrifices in life; she'd learnt that the moment she'd married Roger.

She watched her husband draining his wine glass. He'd had far too much to drink, as usual. A large whisky before they'd left the house – never mind the ones she didn't know about – two more here before dinner, and she'd lost count of the glasses of wine. She'd have to put a stop to it and take him home early after dinner before he made an even greater fool of himself.

"How are you liking Frog End, Colonel?"

He sat down beside the Vicar's wife in the drawing-room after dinner, and balanced his coffee cup and saucer on his knee.

"Everybody keeps asking me that."

"Well, not everybody does – like it. It can be too quiet for some. Specially those who've been used to a more exciting life. Such as yourself."

"I wouldn't say mine had been particularly exciting. I haven't fought in any wars and it's been fairly routine, except for a stint in Northern Ireland."

"I don't envy you that."

"It was only for six months."

"Where else did you serve?"

"Hong Kong, Cyprus, Germany . . . The army are rather running out of places abroad now. I finished up behind a desk at the Ministry of Defence in London doing battle with a mountain of paperwork and attending endless committees."

"And then they retired you? It seems an awful waste."

"Thank you. But there are plenty more where I came from, and the army's shrinking fast."

"Isn't that a mistake? The world's no more stable or safer than it was before the Wall came down, or so it seems to me. In fact, sometimes I think it's worse. At least we knew where we were with the Russians."

"There's some truth in that."

Ruth Swynford came round offering after-dinner mints. The Colonel took one politely but Mrs Beede shook her head.

"I can't eat chocolate," she told him, aside. "It gives me migraine."

He smiled at her. "And I shouldn't eat it."

Her hands, he noticed, were badly affected, the joints red and swollen, the fingers bent, and her lower limbs looked wasted. But she seemed an admirably cheerful and positive person, in spite of her disability, and without a trace of self-pity. He admired that very much.

"Tell me, Colonel" she asked. "Did your wife mind being married to the army?"

He said ruefully, "Well, she never complained – except that she missed the children very much. They were both at boarding school in England and when we were abroad we only saw them in the holidays. That used to upset her. Both of us, in fact."

He thought of Laura putting on a brave face waving goodbye to Marcus and Alison, and the tears she had shed afterwards, and of his own sadness. Mrs Beede was looking at him sympathetically.

"It must have done. I'm sorry I never met her. We would have had something in common straight away – both married to institutions – your wife the army, me the Church." She smiled wryly. "There can be a certain loss of identity, if you're not careful."

He knew exactly what she meant because he had seen it happen to Laura. Army wives were expected to serve the army

## Old Soldiers Never Die

as a sort of extension of their husbands either indirectly or, in the case of senior officers' wives, all too directly. Laura had acted as smiling hostess, ambassadress, secretary, surrogate mother and counsellor to the younger wives and general dogsbody and helpmeet to him in countless ways. He realised it now, more than ever.

He said non-committally, "One learns to adapt . . . or rather, Laura did."

"And so have I. I owe it to William. He married me knowing my condition was probably going to get steadily worse, when he needed a full-time, strong and healthy wife to cope. You've met him already, of course, so you'll know what a sincere and truly dedicated man he is."

"Yes, indeed. I gather you met in London in his former parish?"

"I was doing voluntary work at a Youth Centre in the East End and we got to know each other there. He eventually persuaded me to marry him, though I knew I wouldn't be doing him a favour."

"I'm sure he's never regretted it."

She smiled. "He always says that, but it's an increasing trial. I can't do half the things I should be doing to help him. The village is very kind to us, though, they gave me this electric wheelchair so I can get around more easily. I *can* walk, you know, but it's a slow business and I always find it makes for less fuss and embarrassment on occasions like this if I stay put in my chair. Frog End is a good place to live, you'll find that out, though, like many English villages, we're rather caught in time. Still almost feudal, I think sometimes."

He followed her look across the room to where Lady Swynford was seated on the sofa, feeding the chocolate mints to her poodle. The Major sat beside her, leaning over at an unsteady angle; he reminded the Colonel of a neglected old dog, waiting anxiously for some sign of approval. He turned back to Mrs Beede and encountered her dry gaze. There was a lot more to her than he had first thought, he decided. Her physical movements might be affected, but there was nothing wrong with the sharpness of her observation.

"There's some beautiful countryside round here, Colonel," she went on blandly. "But I expect you've discovered that already."

"Laura and I did a bit of touring in Dorset years ago when we were home on leave, but I haven't explored since then."

"When you feel like it, there's lots to see. William often goes walking along the coast path when he needs to think things out, and in the summer he sometimes swims at Lulworth Cove very early in the morning, before the crowds get there. He finds it very therapeutic."

"I'll remember that," he told her politely. She had summed him up, perfectly accurately, as a lonely widower still mourning his wife but he knew that no amount of walking and swimming would help unless it was to make him tired enough to sleep at night. The doctor's pills knocked him out like a light and left him feeling hungover in the morning, but at least he slept.

He drove the short distance back to the cottage under a full moon that bathed the village green in a cold white light. A badger shambled across in front of the Riley and froze, blinking in the headlights. He stopped to avoid it and saw it lumber off into the shadows.

Silence awaited him in the cottage. The hidden enemy, ready to demoralise and defeat. He took a pill and went to bed, falling into a deep and, mercifully dreamless, sleep.

# Eight

"I've sacked Jacob."

Ruth straightened up from her weeding. "Why on *earth* did you go and do that?"

Her mother had paused on her way back to the house, a trug of 'Queen Elizabeth' roses in one hand, a large straw hat on her head against the hot sun. "He gives me the creeps and I won't have him around any more. I caught him hiding behind the hedge just now, watching me in that barmy way of his. I think he's completely loopy and quite probably unsafe."

"He's perfectly all right, I promise you. Just hopeless with people. And he's a wonderful gardener. I don't know how I'll manage without him."

"You can get someone else."

"Easier said than done. And there's the fête coming up. If you want the garden to look good then I'll need him."

"I've told him he can stay until the end of the month, so he can help with that. After that he must go."

"He'll be dreadfully upset. Poor Jacob."

"I can't help that. I've put up with him for long enough. And speaking of putting up with people, that Rankin woman had the nerve to come here this morning and start telling me I shouldn't have raised her rent. She had the cheek to say that your father wouldn't have wanted it."

Ruth wiped her forehead, leaving a long streak of mud.

"Well he probably wouldn't, would he? He always liked Phillipa and had a lot of respect for her. It was an arrangement between them."

"She's had the use of those paddocks for virtually nothing for years – I can't go on being a charity for ever. Not these days. There's absolutely no reason why she shouldn't pay a fair rent, like everyone else has to – the solicitor completely agrees with me. She tried to tell me that she'd have to close down, but I don't believe a word of it."

"She's not the sort of person to exaggerate, Ma, and I think you ought to reconsider it. She does a pretty good job with that riding school of hers and she takes disabled pupils, too. It's not just to make money."

"There's no need to get so worked up, Ruth."

"Well, I don't think it's fair to undo that arrangement. There's no need for it—"

"I think I should be the judge of that. In any case, I can't stand here in this heat arguing with you."

Ruth watched her mother walk away across the terrace and go through the open French windows into the drawing-room. There wasn't much hope that she would change her mind about either poor Jacob or Phillipa and it was a crying shame in both cases. With a sigh she went back to her weeding. A moment later her mother reappeared at the windows.

"There's a phone call for you, Ruth."

"Who is it?"

"Dr Harvey. He wants a word with you. I can't imagine what about."

She put down her trowel reluctantly, imagining all too well.

"Is that you, Father?"

The Colonel held the receiver away from his ear. For some reason his daughter-in-law always shouted down the phone,

## Old Soldiers Never Die

as though he were stone deaf. And he wished she wouldn't call him Father. He'd never suggested it and 'Hugh' would have done very nicely. Laura hadn't enjoyed being called 'Mother' any better either, but they'd both given up trying to change it.

"Hallo, Susan. How are you all?"

"Oh, we're all right. I'm calling to see how *you* are, Father. You know how we always worry about you."

"There's no need. I'm doing very well. Everything's fine."

"Are you eating a sensible diet?"

"Rather." She was using the nannying tone that so irritated him. After Laura's death she had suddenly started to try and boss him around and behave as though he was not only deaf but senile too.

"We wish you lived nearer, like we wanted," she went on. "Then we could keep a proper eye on you."

He thanked God he'd had the sense not to do any such thing; she would have been round every day with bowls of nourishing soup.

"Alison came down to see me," he said to change the subject.

"Oh, did she?"

From the cool response, it was obviously the wrong thing to say. Susan didn't like Alison any more than Alison liked her. Stupid of him to mention her.

"We'd have been down ourselves sooner but Marcus has been so busy at work, and Eric has had a dreadful cold –"

"I'm quite all right, I assure you."

"As a matter of fact, that was one thing I was ringing about, Father. We thought we'd come and stay next weekend, if that's convenient. We could drive down on Saturday morning."

Much as he wanted to see Marcus, his heart sank at the prospect. "Next weekend . . ." He played for time, wondering if he dared make some excuse, and then remembered that he had one ready made. "I'm afraid next weekend wouldn't be any good – there's a village fête and I'm the new treasurer. It means I'll be tied up there all day."

"Oh." She sounded hurt. "Well, I don't think we'll be able to get down until next month, then."

"Never mind."

"I'll just look at my diary."

There was the sound of pages rustling importantly and he waited.

"We might be able to manage the second weekend of July, Father, if I cancel an engagement."

He succumbed to the inevitable. "That would be fine."

"I'll bring the meals with me, of course. I know you can't manage."

"No need," he told her firmly. "I'm learning to cook."

Afterwards, he went next door. He found Naomi in her greenhouse, watering plants. Mutt and Jeff were panting in the shade and wagged their tails at him without bothering to get up. He stood at the open door of the lean-to. Today his neighbour was sporting emerald-green tracksuit bottoms and an old white T-shirt with the outdated legend BOLLOCKS TO THE POLL TAX written large across the front. He wondered where on earth she had got it and whether she wore it about the village. Very likely.

"I need some simple recipes, Naomi – foolproof ones. My son and his family are coming to stay next month. If I don't show that I can cook, my daughter-in-law will be sending me food parcels for ever."

She guffawed heartlessly. "Like that, is it? I'll look some out for you and you can experiment. How many in the family?"

"They've got a small boy – Eric. He's three."

"What does he eat?"

## Old Soldiers Never Die

"Nothing they want him to," he said, remembering the table tantrums and Susan's losing battles. ('It's very good for you, Eric. You must have your vitamins. Just a little spoonful for Mummy . . .')

"Ah. Well, we'll try to come up with something small boys generally like." She waved her watering can at the rows of plants. "What do you think of this lot? Revolting colours, aren't they, but people love them. The brighter, the better."

He blinked at the garish pinks and reds and purples, some were even striped with white. There was nothing remotely like them in Naomi's own garden. "For your plant stall?"

"That's right. They'll sell like hot cakes. Always do. And people contribute, so I usually end up with plenty. By the way, I've got another plant I've been keeping for you." She emerged from the greenhouse and picked up a pot outside. "Here you are. *Erigeron* 'prosperity'. Useful little chap for the front of your border. Pretty flowers. Treat him well and talk to him kindly and if you give him at least a foot all round he'll soon fill it up for you." She put down the can. "Now, let's go and find those recipes so you can get some practice in."

He followed her into Pear Tree Cottage, his first visit indoors there. The dust and disorder inside showed where Naomi's priorities clearly lay – outside in her garden. The kitchen was a muddle of cooking and gardening things: jars and pans and utensils mixed up with balls of twine, secateurs, and empty flower pots. The sink seemed to be full of unwashed dishes, and the table in the centre was stacked with a pile of old newspapers and plastic plant trays.

"Getting ready for the fête," she said. "Bloody bore, really. Still, it's all in a good cause. Wouldn't want the church roof to fall in." She ran her hand along a shelf of well-used cookery books. "Let's see now. Foolproof and fit for a picky small boy . . ."

He glanced idly at the top of the newspaper pile and saw a large front-page photo of Harold Wilson. The caption read: THE PRIME MINISTER ARRIVING BACK IN LONDON YESTERDAY.

"Good grief, Naomi! This paper's more than twenty years old."

She looked over her shoulder. "Is it? That's nothing. Jessica hoarded everything: string, paper bags, magazines, newspapers. Never threw a thing away. It was the war, I suppose. I chucked most of it out when we moved from the Hall to the cottage, but I kept some of the newspapers because they're handy for lighting fires and wrapping the plants up at the fête. That's what those are for. People don't like carrying them round all muddy and dripping. There's still a whole lot more in the outhouse. I don't bother to buy a daily these days myself. Too pricey and I see the news on television. Besides, it's so depressing – violence, wars, earthquakes, famine, floods – who wants to know?"

"When did you sister die?"

"Three years ago. We'd only been here a few months and she caught a bad cold that winter and went steadily downhill. There was something wrong with her heart, apparently, but we never knew it until then."

"Were you very close?"

"Very. Always had been; since we were kids. When my husband walked out I went back to live at the Hall. Jess had never left it, of course. Never married, or anything. Alan was the love of her life; it nearly killed her when he dumped her for Ursula. We simply couldn't afford to keep the Hall going by then, though, so we sold it for a song to some man who promptly turned the house into flats and sold off most of the garden to a developer. *He* went and built hideous bungalows all over it, as you've probably seen. We'd no idea that would happen." She turned back to the bookshelf again.

## Old Soldiers Never Die

"I looked at one before Pond Cottage – Journey's End."

"I hope you never seriously considered it." She took down a tattered folder that was almost falling apart. "This is my old and trusted file – recipes I've collected since the year dot and that really work. Don't always believe the ones you read in books and magazines, by the way. They often tell you wrong. Too much or too little of something and the wrong time and temperature. These I *know* work." She turned the grease-spotted pages. Some of the recipes, he saw, had been cut out of magazines and stuck in, others were handwritten.

"Here's one for an easy chicken casserole, but your grandson would probably think that was puke. My grandchildren certainly would."

"You have grandchildren?" He was surprised. She'd never mentioned them, or any children, before.

"Two of them. One boy, one girl. I don't see much of them, though. My son emigrated to Australia and married a dyed-in-the-wool sheila out there. Their last visit back here was five years ago and she hated the weather. I've been out once but I can't say I cared for theirs either. Too damn hot." She went on turning pages. "None of these . . . How about good old plain roast chicken? And new potatoes – buy the ones ready scrubbed. You can't go too far wrong with those. And here's a nice chocolate pud that's a doddle. I'll write it all down for you."

She unearthed a piece of paper and pencil from somewhere amid the chaos and scrawled out instructions. "There you are. And I'd get some fish fingers and frozen peas in, if I were you, and some of those frozen chips that you can just stick in the oven. And the most lurid-looking ice cream you can find. Oh, and don't forget a bottle of ketchup. He'll love you for it."

She had written it all down on the back of an old bill and he glanced through it quickly.

Rost Chicken: Heat oven to 375°. Put chicken in rosting tin and smeer well with softened butter or margerine. Cook twenty minutes to the pound and twenty minutes over.
New potatos: Boil in salted water until just cooked and drain.
Choclate Moose: melt choclate and butter in a bowl in oven. Seperate whites from yokes . . .

He thanked her, hiding his amusement, and went away thinking what a marvellous tonic Naomi was.

"Do you know the Brace of Pheasants at Plush?"
Ruth shook her head. "I don't think so. I don't remember it."
"Because that's where we're going. Very off the beaten track but worth it when you get there."
She stared out of the car window, not much caring where they went. If it hadn't been for Mama mouthing and grimacing her disapproval while she was taking the phone call from Dr Harvey she would never have agreed to this outing in the first place. As soon as she had put the receiver down, her mother had started.
"Do you mean he was actually asking you out, Ruth? What colossal impertinence!"
"I don't quite see why."
"I do. I invite him to dinner once and apparently he thinks that's some sign of social acceptance. Those sort of people always have an eye for the main chance."
"I'm hardly a main chance."
"He's no fool. He knows there must be money about, and how frail my health is—"
"For heavens sake, Ma! That's plain *ridiculous*."

## Old Soldiers Never Die

"Well, I'm telling you, you shouldn't have anything to do with him."

"It's really not for you to say, is it? I'm thirty-five and old enough to go out with whom I please."

And so, here she was, going out with whom she actually didn't please. She sat in silence while he drove the car along narrow and then still narrower lanes, deeper and deeper into the Dorset countryside, thoroughly vexed at having let herself be goaded into the situation.

The Brace of Pheasants, when they finally reached it, turned out to be worth the journey and plenty of other people obviously thought so too because it was crowded.

"I hope you're hungry," he told her. "The food's good."

"Do you come here a lot, then?"

"I don't get much time, unless I make it. Running a one-man practice doesn't leave much over."

Tom smiled at her and he had a nice smile. She'd never really noticed before. There shouldn't be any shortage of women queueing up. It was supposed to be an occupational hazard for doctors, wasn't it? Vicars, too, though she couldn't quite imagine William Beede being pursued by bands of yearning females.

He said, "This is a treat for me – though it may not be for you."

"I'm sorry. I didn't mean to seem rude."

"You didn't. Now, what are you going to have to eat?"

During the meal she kept the conversation general, innocuous chat between virtual strangers, but towards the end he said in his direct way.

"Will you come out with me again?"

"I don't think there'd be much point."

"I'll risk it, if you will."

She smiled, but she didn't intend to. She didn't want to get involved with him, or with anyone else. Not now, not yet, and probably never again.

# Nine

When the Colonel woke up on the morning of the village fête he saw that it was going to be the sort of glorious summer's day that made people wonder why anyone could ever leave England: one of those that made up for all the bad ones. The sky was cloudless blue, the sun already hot, and the view across the green from his bedroom window was enough to raise anyone's spirits. For once the sleeping pill hadn't left him groggy and he felt fresh and alert; he even whistled as he shaved.

By the time he reached the Manor, preparations were well in progress: trestle tables being taken onto the large back lawn, stalls set up and goods laid out. He came across Miss Butler dragging a tabletop along by herself and hurried to help her.

"Oh, thank you *so* much, Colonel. It's for the cake stall. I'm a sort of roving pair of hands, you see." She insisted on hanging on to one end and they carried the table top across the lawn between them, with the tin petty-cash box that he had brought with him balanced on the top. He was surprised at her strength, but then, though she was small, she was wiry, and no doubt her years in the navy had left her with a healthy physique. He set the tabletop on the two trestles for her and left her shaking out a starched white tablecloth.

Ruth Swynford came up, carrying a plant wrapped in

newspaper. "Good morning, Colonel. Aren't we lucky with the weather? I'll show you where your treasurer's office is." She led him into the house via a side door at the east end, and down a stone-flagged passageway into the back part of the hall.

"In here, Colonel." She opened a door to a panelled snuggery with a big leather-topped desk and a great many books on shelves. "This was my father's study. He used to spend a lot of time in here."

He looked at the room's womb-like comfort and wasn't surprised.

"Is there anything else you need?" she asked.

He saw that she had put out the accounts book, a pocket calculator, ballpoint pens, pencils, sharpener, eraser, notepad, elastic bands, paperclips, small ziplock bags.

"You seem to have thought of everything. Thank you."

She smiled at him. "I was a secretary in my other life. I'm just general dogsbody today and it's my job to go round the stalls every so often collecting the takings from them so you can get on with the counting during the afternoon, rather than having to do it all at the end."

"That'll be a great help."

"Would you like me to take round the floats? We usually give each stall about ten pounds in change to start them off."

"No, I'll do it, thank you all the same. Familiarise myself with it all."

"If you see anything you want, you can buy it before we're officially open at two and the rush starts. We don't get much of a chance after that. Perks for the committee members." She showed him the plant she was carrying, pulling aside the newspaper wrapping. "I got this from Naomi's stall."

He was relieved to see that it was something with white flowers, not one of the gaudy horrors.

## Old Soldiers Never Die

She put the plant down on the windowsill. "I'll open the window for you, Colonel. It'll get pretty hot in here, facing south."

As she pushed the lattice window open the sounds of the frenzied activity outside on the lawn filtered in, including voices upraised in bitter argument. Ruth Swynford sighed. "Oh dear, trouble. There always is."

Before she could leave the room heavy footsteps sounded in the hall and Mrs Bentley appeared in the doorway, flushed and furious.

"There you are, Ruth. Can you come at once, please? Major Cuthbertson has taken an extra table which means we're only left with two for cakes. He *refuses* to hand it over. He's only supposed to have one for bottles, as you know. It was all agreed at the committee meeting."

"I'll come and sort it out, Mrs Bentley."

She gave him a wry look as she went and he didn't envy her the job. In the hurry she had forgotten the plant.

He sat down at Sir Alan Swynford's desk and counted out the ten pound floats, putting the coins into ziplock plastic bags. When he had done that he went outside again onto the lawn where considerable progress had been made. The stalls looked almost ready and he could see Mr Townsend putting the final touches to the hoop-la at the far corner of the lawn. Jacob, he noticed, was clipping away at the tall hedge behind it, like a scene painter making last-minute adjustments to a backdrop before the curtain goes up. And what a backdrop! A beautiful English country house garden in the full and lovely bloom of mid-summer.

He went round the stalls distributing his plastic bags of coins. At the cake stall, Mrs Bentley and Mrs Thompson, with Miss Butler's help, were still fussing over their spread of home-made offerings, carefully shaded from the sun by big garden umbrellas. He admired the array of cakes and biscuits and gingerbread and meringues and flapjacks before moving on to Mrs Warner who was busy arranging and re-arranging an eclectic jumble of bric-a-brac, her heavy silver earrings a-jangle, and then to Mrs Latimer who had finished sorting her second-hand books and was deeply engrossed in a paperback entitled *Desire under the Moon*. The cover had a colourful picture of a sheikh carrying off a flowing-haired, half-naked woman in his arms. She put it down hurriedly, blushing.

"Anything I can sell you, Colonel? I've got some military history somewhere."

She rummaged through a pile and produced a mildewed volume on the siege of Khartoum. For the sake of politeness and the church roof, he bought it.

He found Naomi swearing and struggling with an improvised awning for her stall.

"The plants'll go and wilt on me if I don't give them some shade. Lend us a hand, Hugh."

He helped her fix the canvas into place and gave her her float before passing on to Major Cuthbertson and his bottle stall, who must have lost his battle with Mrs Bentley. The single table before him was crammed with bottles of every description.

"No damn room," the Major told him bitterly. "That Bentley battleaxe pinched my other one for her silly cakes."

"You've got a pretty good selection."

"Supposed to be all booze, but some people are so damned mean they'll give anything." He held up a bottle of lemonade in disgust and plonked it down. "Want a go? Only ten pence a time."

He siezed hold of the handle of the wooden drum beside him and cranked it furiously. The Colonel had ten goes at pulling out a number corresponding with one on the stall and, on the last, won a small bottle of tabasco sauce.

## Old Soldiers Never Die

"What did I tell you," the Major said morosely. "Not worth the bloody effort."

At the far end of the lawn Jacob had finished his hedge clipping and was nowhere to be seen, but Mr Townsend was aiming rope quoits at posts spaced out on the grass.

"Ah, Colonel, I wonder if you'd give it a try? I want to make sure it's not too easy for them."

"How does it work?"

"Well, each post is numbered, as you see. You have six quoits and the idea is to ring posts that will add up to over fifty. The higher the number, the further away, of course. And you have to stand behind the chalk line."

"And if I get more than fifty?"

"Then you win a prize." Mr Townsend waved his hand proudly towards a table set in the shade of the tall hedge. "You can choose any one you wish. Come and take a look. They're all contributions, you know – a lot of them hand made. Some of our ladies are very talented."

He fervently hoped he wouldn't be faced with the delicate problem of choosing between various knitted toys, a quilted satin hot-water bottle cover, pink bedsocks, Devon Violets bathsalts, a crocheted blanket, a heart-shaped cellophane box of chocolates tied up with a red bow, an arrangement of dried flowers sprouting out of a block of highly varnished wood, a crinolined lady concealing a roll of lavatory paper in her mauve tiered skirts.

He lobbed the quoits in the general direction of the posts and to his relief scored only twenty-eight. Mr Townsend collected them up, looking pleased.

"Not as simple as it looks, eh, Colonel? Sorry you missed out on a prize."

The silver band was assembling below the terrace as he walked back to the house, arranging their chairs in crescent form and setting up their music stands. They were nearly all young, he noticed, some only teenagers and several of them girls.

He returned to the study where the sun was pouring in and and opened the window wider. Ruth's plant, still on the sill, was drooping unhappily and the soil looked bone dry so he moved it into the small patch of shade cast by the stone embrasure and sat down at the desk. He took another look through the past accounts in the book. It was all quite straightforward. The takings from each stall and attraction were entered, plus the gate money, and the grand total was set against the outgoings for printing posters, hiring the band, Portaloos, insurance, and so on. Last year the fête had made eight hundred and thirty-seven pounds, net.

"How nice to see you again, Colonel. No, please don't get up."

He had risen to his feet at the sight of Lady Swynford framed in the doorway. She was wearing something soft and flowing in the colour of clotted cream. A matching scarf trailed from a hand that also held a bag of the same colour, and the other hand was lifted to touch the door jamb lightly. Her scent drifted towards him, something expensively French. Again, as at the committee meeting, he was reminded of an actress making an entrance on stage. And he guessed that it was her first public appearance of the day. She moved into the room and her poodle followed her. It sniffed at his shoes and looked up at him with liquidly bright eyes that had no particular expression.

"This was my late husband's study, you know."

"I hope you don't mind it being used."

"Not at all. Frankly, I could never understand why Alan liked it in here so much – so small and poky, and so hot in summer." She fanned herself lightly with the scarf. "You

## Old Soldiers Never Die

should take your jacket off, Colonel, you'd be much more comfortable."

"Perhaps later."

She looked at him sideways. "Quite a stickler for standards, aren't you? I so admire that. The way the people dress these days is appalling, don't you agree? Anything goes."

A dancer, hadn't Naomi said? But what kind? Ballet? No, she was rather too tall and the wrong type. A high-kicking chorus girl to Sir Alan's stage-door Johnnie? It didn't seem likely. A sort of Isadora Duncan, then, floating round the stage and fluttering a scarf like she was doing now. The large diamond-spray brooch pinned to her left shoulder glittered in the sunlight from the window. Even in her role as lady of the manor she was absurdly over-dressed for a village fête.

"It's a changing world," he observed mildly.

"It is, indeed. And for the worse, in my opinion. Do sit down, Colonel. I'm on my way out. I have to make my little speech in a while – opening the fête, you know. Rather a bore, but it's expected."

He started to sit down and then remembered something. He fetched the plant from windowsill.

"Your daughter left this behind Lady Swynford. I'm afraid it's wilting badly but I wasn't quite sure what to do about it."

She frowned down at the drooping plant in its dusty newspaper wrapping. "What a nuisance of her. I suppose I'd better take it and give it some water."

She took it from him gingerly, holding it well away from the cream chiffon. For two pins, he guessed, she wouldn't have bothered but for the fact that she wanted his admiration. She gave a little laugh. "I'm afraid I'm not a gardener, Colonel, are you?"

He met her eyes, raised conspiratorially to his. "No, Lady Swynford. But I'm learning."

\* \* \*

Ruth was on her first round of the stalls and the stallholders were reluctant to surrender their takings. They liked to see the bowls filling up, not being emptied, and she realised that they didn't trust her not to muddle them up with other stalls. Between cakes and plants, she ran straight into Dr Harvey. He was carrying a hand-knitted toy elephant.

"I just won it at the hoop-la," he told her, dangling it by its trunk.

"What on earth are you going to do with it?"

"It'll be useful in the surgery waiting room. We keep a box of toys there for the kids."

She'd heard that he was very good with the children. Mrs Hunt's daughter, for one, swore by him for her Sharon.

The band was launching into an unsteady rendering of 'Born Free' as she walked on. She could see her mother making a royal progress across the lawn with Shoo-Shoo in attendance, stopping to say a few words here and there. The sun was really very hot, beating down on the scene. I hope nobody goes and faints on us, she thought, and was rather glad that Dr Harvey was around.

She finished the collection and took her plastic boxes towards the house.

"Ruth! My God, *Ruth!* What are *you* doing here?"

Her heart lurched at the sound of the voice she knew so well. She turned slowly in its direction, feeling dizzy with shock. It's me that's going to faint in a minute, she thought, if I don't get a bloody grip on myself. He was standing a few feet away, staring at her in embarrassed astonishment.

"I live here, Ralph."

"*Here*? In this house?"

He was looking puzzled now, as well as amazed. But then of course he wouldn't have known. All he'd ever known about her was that her parents lived somewhere in Dorset. He'd

## Old Soldiers Never Die

never written to her here, or phoned her, or been any part of her life other than the one she had lived in her London flat. She could hardly have brought him here with her on her occasional weekend visits: "This is my lover, Ralph. He has a wife and two children and has been married for almost twenty-five years, but we don't let that worry us."

"It belongs to my mother."

She could see that he hadn't expected her to come from quite such an impressive background. He must have pictured her going back to something far more modest in the country, not a Jacobean mansion. It seemed extraordinary now that they'd never talked about her home. Only about his.

"Good heavens! I'd no idea . . ."

"I might ask you the same question," she said. "What on earth are *you* doing here?"

"We're staying with friends nearby. They suggested it. I think they come every year. Said it was rather amusing." He'd stopped looking so surprised, and was only slightly embarrassed. "Look, Ruth, could we talk somewhere?"

"I don't think there's anything to talk about, is there?"

"Yes there is." He took a step towards her and lowered his voice. "The fact is I've missed you like hell. I wish to God we'd never split up. It was a crazy thing to do."

"Actually, you said it was the only sensible thing to do."

"I know. And I thought it was then. For both of us. For *all* of us. It wasn't easy for me, you know."

"It wasn't very easy for me either."

"I'm sorry. Believe me, Ruth, I've regretted it over since." He glanced around quickly. "Helen's somewhere with our friends. I'll have to go and find them, but couldn't we meet somewhere in a while – somewhere away from everyone? I want to talk to you. Just for a moment."

He'd put on some weight: he was a little heavier round the

jaw and a little greyer, too, otherwise he was just the same. And having the same effect on her in spite of all her good resolutions.

"There's a path beside the stable block where they're selling teas, and it leads round to the kitchen gardens. I'll meet you there by the greenhouses in half an hour."

He looked at her intently. "I'll be there."

In the hall she encountered her mother.

"Who was that man you were talking to, darling?"

"Just someone I used to know in London."

"Attractive. You've never talked about him."

"There's nothing to say."

"You were always so secretive about your London life, Ruth. I wonder what you *did* get up to.

"I worked."

"Not all the time. You know, it's really quite surprising how secrets can be kept for years."

"What exactly are you driving at?"

"Don't be so prickly, darling. I wasn't really referring to you. I'm going upstairs to lie down for a while. The heat out there's appalling and I've got the most *dreadful* headache. I'll stay there until all those awful people have gone."

"What about announcing the raffle winners? And guess the weight? You usually do that."

"Someone else will have to – Mrs Cuthbertson can. She won't even need a loudspeaker . . . I'm feeling quite exhausted."

"Sure you're all right? I could fetch Dr Harvey."

"Not *him*, thank you. Come along Shoo-Shoo."

She watched her mother go up the stairs, Shoo-Shoo at her heels, and wondered if she should consult with Tom Harvey nonetheless. But her mother looked quite well and it probably was just the heat.

\* \* \*

## Old Soldiers Never Die

The Major ducked down below the level of his table and took a swig at the half bottle of vodka he'd left propped carefully against the trestle leg. He re-emerged, wiping his mouth quickly and looked round to see if anyone had noticed. Nobody had. There was a lull at the bottle stall which had given him the chance. Since the only bottle of whisky had been won (by the *Vicar* of all people), nobody was quite so keen on having a go, and he couldn't blame them. Couldn't stand vodka himself, didn't taste of anything, but needs must when the devil drives – whatever that meant. And he'd won the half bottle fair and square. He'd had to buy nearly forty goes to do it, but he'd given the drum a good turning and closed his eyes when he'd put his hand inside. No cheating. Never had cheated in his life. Not the thing at all. Of course, he'd had his eye on the bottle of Teacher's, like everybody else, but at least he'd got spirits of a kind, and not the British sherry, or that home-made damson wine muck. And one good thing about vodka was that you couldn't smell it on someone's breath – so people said.

He look round again and dived down for another quick nip. Fact was, he needed a bit of a stiffener just now, so what the hell? Bit of a body blow he'd taken. Surely she hadn't meant it, though? He must have been mistaken. The old hearing wasn't what it used to be and that damned band had been blasting away – some bloody pop tune – they hadn't played a decent march all afternoon. He must have misheard. He'd have gone right after her when she walked off if only he hadn't been tied to this bloody silly stall. Yes, he'd've had it out with her. Put it to her straight. Where did he stand? A cat may look at a king. Or a king may look at a cat.

God, there was Marjorie coming across the lawn. He kicked the vodka bottle further under the trestle table. Well, one good thing, he could ask the old girl to take over for a bit, so he could get away. Sort things out. Man to woman. He straightened himself up, shoulders back, chin up, and hoped it was true about vodka.

The takings were mounting up steadily. The Colonel double-checked the latest from pony rides and made a note. Then he ate the cucumber sandwich and the iced fairy cake and drank the cup of tea that Ruth Swynford had thoughtfully brought him earlier. She had left the study door open to give him some more air and he was vaguely aware of the odd person passing by. Through the open window he could hear the goings-on on the lawn: the buzz of a crowd's talk and laughter, children shouting, a baby crying, megaphone announcements made by Mrs Cuthbertson from the terrace *fortissimo con vibrato*, and the periodic bursts of activity from the silver band who had just ground to the end of 'Don't Cry for Me, Argentina'. He winced as they swung into 'June is Bustin' Out All Over'.

"Pretty awful, aren't they?" Naomi came into the room, carrying a plastic bowl full of coins and notes. She dumped it on the desk. "Ruth hasn't been round for a while so I thought I'd bring it in myself. I've left someone else in charge for a bit. Needed a break and the loo. How about you?"

He smiled. "No, I'm fine."

"How are we doing with the takings?"

"Very well, I'd say. Looks like we'll break last year's record."

"That's good. The Vicar'll be pleased. Well, I can't wait any longer and I'm not queuing at the Portaloos just to please dear Ursula."

He had just finished counting the plant stall takings when he heard an odd humming sound outside the door and Jean Beede manoeuvred her electric wheelchair skilfully into the room.

"I've come to see if I can help you, Colonel. Make myself a bit useful." She took in his surprised expression. "I can get

*Old Soldiers Never Die*

around very well in this on my own, you see. William just helped me in over the steps and I can do all the rest. Would you like me to guard everything while you stretch your legs?"

She had put it more delicately than Naomi and now that he thought about it, it wasn't such a bad idea.

"If you wouldn't mind."

"I'll do some counting for you, if you like."

He indicated the latest plant stall contribution arranged in neat piles of coins "Well, you could check this lot, if you feel like it. See if we get the same answer."

"I'd be glad to." She held up a bottle of Teacher's whisky that had been wedged beside her in the chair. "Look what William won at the bottle stall."

"Lucky chap."

"He was quite embarrassed, poor William. Didn't want to carry it around with him. People don't think Vicars should drink whisky, for some reason, you know."

"So he told me."

"He's often lucky at those sort of things. He won something at the hoop-la, too. I never seem to win anything at all." She smiled at him. "Well, I'll get started. Don't hurry back. I'll be perfectly happy."

He helped her position her wheelchair close up to the front of the desk and left her starting to re-count the plant takings. When he had found and made use of the downstairs cloakroom, hoping Lady Swynford wasn't around, he wandered out into the lawn.

"Why have you done this, Ruth?"

"Done what?"

Ralph gestured vaguely round the kitchen garden, at the rows of potatoes and beans and lettuces. "Buried yourself here, in the depths of the country."

"My mother had a stroke. She's a widow and I came to take care of her."

She noticed that he kept looking round to make sure they weren't observed, even though they were well out of sight behind the wall.

"But she's well again now, isn't she? That was her opening the fête, wasn't it? She looked perfectly all right."

"She's recovered, yes. And I've discovered that I like being buried in the country. I've taken up gardening – rather seriously, as a matter of fact."

"You mean you won't come back to London?"

"Why on earth should I? There's nothing for me there."

"Surely your work . . ."

"It meant nothing to me. This does."

"Don't I mean something to you still, though? *I'm* there."

"Not any longer. That's what you decided."

He put up his hands. "I know. I know. And I was wrong. Utterly and completely wrong. But I did honestly think I was doing the right thing for everyone. It took a lot to say that to you, you know. I felt an absolute heel—"

"You *were* an absolute heel. You should have said it long before. But then I should have broken it off myself long before, too. I don't blame you, Ralph, if that's a comfort. It was just as much my fault. And you were quite right – it *was* the best thing. You've saved your marriage and I'm rebuilding my life. We've got to stick to that."

"God, I miss you, though . . . you know how it's always been with Helen. I haven't loved her for years. Can't think why I ever married her in the first place. I could have had you – *Christ!* There's someone over there, watching us."

She turned. "It's only Jacob. He's the gardener. Don't worry, he won't say anything. He never talks to anyone if he can help it."

## Old Soldiers Never Die

"Are you sure?"

"Quite sure. He wouldn't have a clue who you are, and he's gone now, anyway."

He looked relieved and smiled his old smile at her: the one that had always melted her heart. "Do you know, Ruth, I scarcely recognised you just now. You've changed so much. You look quite different. Clothes, hair . . . well, everything."

"I like me better this way."

"I like you this way, too," he said. "I like the suntan and the freckles. As a matter of fact it's all extremely attractive."

"It isn't meant to be."

"I realise that – that's the irony. So, there's no one else, then? No other man in your life, who's taken my place?"

"No."

He took a step towards her and put his hands on her shoulders. "There's no reason why we couldn't meet sometimes, is there, Ruth? Whenever we could manage it? You could come up to London or, better still, I could come down here. We could stay at some nice old pub – have several days together, just the two of us . . ."

I've got to be strong, she thought. I've simply *got* to be strong.

The Colonel came across Miss Butler trying to guess the weight of a cake.

"Are you going to have a go here, Colonel?"

"I'm not very good on things like this. No idea at all."

"Oh, that doesn't matter. You just guess anything and write it down, with your name and address and phone number. At the end of the day whoever guessed the closest wins the cake."

"Supposing it's a tie?"

She gave a little trill. "I expect they cut it in two."

He looked doubtfully at the iced cake. It sat in state on a silver stand and was decorated with sugar pink roses all round its base and rim and with a much bigger rose in the centre that had shiny green angelica leaves. He remembered eating some angelica as a child at a birthday party and hating the taste. There was no way of knowing what it was made of inside – light sponge or heavy fruit – so any guess was a stab in the dark. He hadn't a clue how much cakes weighed anyway. He wrote down three pounds, six ounces.

The band was taking a merciful tea break while he wandered about some more and bought raffle tickets and a brass letter opener from bric-a-brac. He passed the sign pointing to the pony rides that were taking place in a small paddock somewhere out of sight beyond the tall hedge at the end of the lawn. Mrs Cuthbertson was manning the bottle stall in the Major's place and he had several more tries and won a bottle of Schweppes tonic water. Naomi was back behind her stall.

"Don't buy anything," she advised him. "Any decent stuff's gone and you'll hate these colours."

"I'd like to, though. It's in a good cause."

"All right. How about this one?"

He looked at the flowerless plant. "What is it?"

"Mint. Plant it in a big pot, or a tub, or something, or it'll spread everywhere. You can use it with your new potatoes." She wrapped it up in newspaper for him. "You should start a herb garden near the back door, Hugh. No good cook should ever be without one."

He tried to sidle past the hoop-la stall but Mr Townsend spotted him.

"Another go, Colonel? Not much left in the way of prizes, I'm afraid."

The crinoline lady remained. So did the dried flower arrangement and the Devon Violets bathsalts. He aimed the quoits wildly but to his dismay his score was fifty-one. Mr Townsend beamed as he chose the dried flowers.

*Old Soldiers Never Die*

"My wife made that, Colonel. Clever, isn't it? We've got a house full of them."

He went back towards the side entrance to the house, carrying the mint, and nearly bumped into the Major who was hurrying out and brushed past him blindly, without a word.

Nasty little tyke, Phillipa Rankin, thought, watching a lout of a boy digging his heels into poor old Petal's sides and flapping his arms like a rodeo clown. Ears back, Petal took off suddenly and cantered briskly down the paddock. The boy flopped around wildly and then slid off sideways. When she reached him he was snivelling and complaining in the grass.

"Threw me off, 'orrible animal."

"She didn't. You fell off and it was entirely your own fault. You told me you could ride. And what on earth were you doing careering off like that?"

"I'm 'urt," he whined.

She looked him over with long experience. "Nothing more than a bruise or two. You're perfectly fine, so you can stop moaning and get up."

The next child was a tearful little girl in a frilly party frock whose mother had persuaded her that she wanted a ride.

"Go *on*, Lorraine. I've paid for you. Don't be such a baby. The lady'll hold on to you."

God preserve me from stupid mothers, she thought, leading Petal at a gentle walk across the paddock, and talking quietly to the child who had a hammerlock on Petal's mane. She put one arm round her comfortingly.

The ponies were getting tired and so was she. After this go she'd take a break and they could have a rest in the shade. She needed the loo as well and her throat was parched so she could find a drink of water at the same time. She turned the pony round at the end of the paddock and started slowly back, still talking to the child and encouraging her all the way. By the time they'd reached the mother, the little girl was patting Petal's neck and smiling. The old magic had worked again. It nearly always did. It was all just a question of building confidence. Encouraging, never forcing. Patience, not rush. She had the capacity for it because she truly cared . . . But what did it matter, anyway? She wouldn't be able to carry on much longer.

The shadows were getting longer across the lawn and the crowds drifting away. Much to the Colonel's relief, the band had packed up and left so that he could get on with the final count without distraction.

The cake sat on a corner of the desk beside Mrs Townsend's dried flower arrangement. To his embarrassment and dismay he had guessed its weight correctly, to the nearest ounce, and Mrs Cuthbertson who had megaphoned the result loudly enough for him to hear it in the study, and for most of Dorset to hear it too, had carried it in to him triumphantly.

"There you are, Colonel. You lucky man!"

He didn't know what he was going to do with the wretched thing. He never ate cake these days – hadn't for years – but maybe it would come in useful when Marcus and Susan came.

The grand total so far was one thousand and fifty-four pounds, sixty-two pence, and there was probably still a bit more to come from some of the stalls. Not bad.

"*Colonel* . . ."

He looked up. Ruth Swynford was standing in the doorway and he saw at once that something was badly wrong. She was very pale and clinging to the post for support. He got to his feet quickly and went to her side.

"It's my mother," she said. "I think she's dead."

\* \* \*

## Old Soldiers Never Die

Dr Harvey drew back from examining Lady Swynford. "Nothing to be done. I'm afraid, Colonel. She's been dead for about an hour, I'd say."

Both men looked down at the still form on the bed. Ursula Swynford was fully clothed, except for her shoes which lay untidily beside the bed, apparently kicked off. Her head rested on a lace-edged pillow, and her arms were by her sides. The folds of her chiffon gown fanned out gracefully on each side, like some Sleeping Beauty, and as though she had staged her final exit as carefully as she had staged her entrances. She looked a good deal softer in death than she had done in life, the Colonel thought, and a great deal better than most other dead bodies that he had seen – the two young subalterns whose jeep had triggered a booby-trap, for example; the woman with her legs blown off in a shopping-precinct bomb explosion; the hostage finally found, too late, in a car boot. She looked as though she were simply asleep, an illusion reinforced by the poodle who was still lying at her feet, muzzle on paws, watching them with its strangely expressionless eyes. Once or twice it licked its lips.

"I imagine she had another stroke Doctor?"

"I assumed so at first, but I'm not sure." The doctor bent closer to the body again. He straightened up after a moment. "Not sure at all, in fact. There are definite signs of petechial haemorrhaging on the neck and face."

"Which means?"

"It means that she didn't go quietly, Colonel. She fought for breath and for life."

Their eyes met. "In what way exactly?"

"Well, she could have choked on something. A chocolate, for instance, which lodged in the trachea." He indicated the open box of chocolates on the bedside table. "It happens and there was nobody around to do anything to help. And it could have happened when she had the stroke, all at the same time. It's possible."

The Colonel moved closer and saw that two chocolates were missing from the box.

"That could account for the haemorrhaging?"

"It could, yes." The doctor started to close his bag. "But I'm afraid they'll have to be an autopsy and I'll have to notify the police. I can't issue a death certificate without further investigation as to the exact cause of death."

The Colonel glanced around the room. Lady Swynford's scarf and handbag lay on the stool before the dressing table. He noted the bottles of expensive scent, the silver-backed brush and hand mirror, a crystal vase of pink roses, a box of tissues, and a pair of spectacles that he guessed vanity kept out of sight as much as possible. Through the open bedroom windows he could hear Mrs Cuthbertson's voice ringing across the lawn, "Where've you been hiding, Roger? Come and give a hand here, chop-chop . . ." The clearing-up was still going on and nobody had any idea what had happened, as yet. Ruth had collapsed into the chair in his study, begging him to find Dr Harvey, and he had left her there and raced outside just in time to catch him as he was leaving.

He said, "Her daughter's waiting down in the study. Would you like me to have a word with her?"

Doctor Harvey shook his head. "I'll speak to her. Could you do something with the dog? Get it out of here?"

The Colonel picked up the poodle and tucked it under his arm. Its breath smelled of chocolate and its fur of the scent that he recognised as the one Lady Swynford had been wearing. It kept wagging its pom-pom tail at him. The brainless animal didn't seem to have registered that its mistress was dead.

# Ten

The man standing at the door of Pond Cottage offered his identification.

"Detective Inspector Squibb, Dorset Police, sir." He indicated the second man standing just behind him. "And this is Detective Sergeant Biddlecombe. We're making inquiries into the death of Lady Swynford of Frog End Manor and we'd like to ask you a few questions, if it's convenient."

The Colonel showed them into the sitting-room. "Please sit down."

The Inspector took the wing-back chair while the Sergeant lowered himself heavily onto one end of the sofa. Thursday, curled up at the other end, lifted his head and glared at him. The Colonel remained standing.

"How can I help you?"

"You may have heard that the coroner's inquest on Lady Swynford's death was opened and then adjourned, pending police investigations?"

He looked young for the job, and cocky with it, the Colonel thought (or was it just that he himself was getting older and less confident?). He was sharply dressed in a light-grey suit, white shirt, silk tie and good shoes and his short-clipped hair was no rustic pudding-basin job but the work of trendier scissors. His accent belonged to nowhere in particular. Sergeant Biddlecome fitted the Colonel's notion of a country plain clothes policeman far better. He was an older man – ruddy faced and rather rumpled and his rich-sounding, "Thank you, sir," as he had entered the room, belonged firmly to Dorset. I'm turning into an old fogey, the Colonel thought ruefully. Resenting the young.

"I read so in the newspaper."

"Lady Swynford had already suffered one stroke and Dr Harvey concluded at first that she had probably suffered a second or possibly choked to death on something she'd eaten. However, the autopsy showed that neither was the case. She hadn't choked on anything, she'd been suffocated."

"*Suffocated*, Inspector?"

"She was smothered with the pillow she was lying on, Colonel. The lab report told us that the linen case bears traces of her saliva and of the lipstick she was wearing and blood from where her teeth had torn her inside lip. And there were fragments of the pillow's lace edging under her nails where she clutched at it in her fight for life. In other words, sir, Lady Swynford was murdered."

The Colonel sat down slowly. "I see. Good God . . . That's terrible. What a dreadful thing for her daughter. Were there any clues? Other traces?"

"You mean of the assailant? The lab couldn't turn up anything. You see, she would have instinctively grabbed hold of the pillow to get it away from her face. All the murderer had to do was hold it down hard and keep out of her reach."

"A man, presumably."

"Not necessarily. A strong and determined woman could have done it quite easily – not very difficult with a rather frail victim of that age."

"Do you have a suspect?"

"Not as yet. The constable on duty was busy directing traffic outside the Manor and according to the gate receipts nearly five hundred people attended the fête at the Manor that day. They had practically all gone home by the time Lady Swynford was found. We appealed to people to come forward but not more than a handful have bothered to do so."

"Not very public spirited of the rest."

"But very normal. People don't usually want to get involved in a police investigation. It's time consuming and a nuisance. They convince themselves they wouldn't be of any use – that there'll be plenty of other witnesses. Not always true, of course, and the smallest clue can be vital. The only names we have of those definitely present are those of officials and stallholders and others who can be verified as attending." The Inspector paused. "Such as yourself."

"That's correct. I'm treasurer of the fête committee."

It sounded like some comical Gilbert and Sullivan character, the Colonel realised as he spoke.

"So we understand. We also understand from Miss Ruth Swynford, Lady Swynford's daughter, that you were the first person she spoke to when she discovered the body of her mother at approximately six p.m. and that you then fetched Dr Harvey who happened to be attending the fête and accompanied him upstairs to Lady Swynford's bedroom?"

"That's correct," he repeated. "Dr Harvey examined Lady Swynford to confirm that she was dead. I had already told him what Miss Swynford said to me – that her mother had been complaining of a headache and had gone to lie down earlier in the afternoon. She thought it was another stroke and so did Dr Harvey, until he examined the body more closely."

"Is there anything you can add to that, sir? Anything you noticed at that time that struck you?"

He thought for a moment. "I remember thinking that her clothing looked very carefully arranged. Rather oddly so."

The Inspector nodded grimly. "Whoever murdered her also

re-arranged the pillow nicely, too, sir. What about the dog? Miss Swynford says that the dog definitely went upstairs with her mother at about three fifteen and that it always stayed with her, on her bed. She told us that when she went in the bedroom to see her mother and found her dead, the dog was lying at her feet."

"That's right. It was still there when Doctor Harvey and I went in."

"Didn't that strike you as odd, too?"

He didn't care for the man's faintly sarcastic tone. "Not particularly. Don't dogs usually stay with their owners, especially if they sense trouble of some kind?"

"In my experience they don't lie quietly. They make some kind of fuss. Show anxiety. Run around."

"I don't think it's a very intelligent dog, Inspector."

"But even stupid dogs generally do something when their owner is being attacked, wouldn't you agree? Even if they don't actually attack the attacker. According to Miss Swynford her mother went up to rest at about a quarter past three. As treasurer, you spent most of the time in the small study off the inner hall. Did you hear the noise of the dog barking upstairs at any time during the afternoon?"

"I don't recall it. The band was playing a lot of the time and I'm not sure I would have been able to hear it anyway."

The Sergeant was taking careful notes, he saw, scribbling away in a spiral bound notepad. Inspector Squibb waited for a moment, presumably for him to catch up.

"Miss Swynford tells us that her mother's dog is very aggressive with strangers. He barks at them loudly until he's called off. But that once he understands that someone is accepted then he never barks at them again."

"I've experienced that myself."

The Inspector grimaced. "So have I. The dog has a very

## Old Soldiers Never Die

shrill, high-pitched bark and a continuous one. Unless it had been told to stop, I think you, or someone would have heard it – the bedroom windows were open, apparently, and give directly onto the main lawn. It suggests that the person who entered the room and murdered Lady Swynford was known both to her and to the dog. That would explain why the dog didn't bark at that point. It still doesn't explain, though, why he didn't bark later when his mistress was being suffocated and fighting for her life. As I said, even a stupid dog should have reacted in some way, even if only in fear. From what I hear, it seemed to be quite unmoved."

"How long would it take to smother someone with a pillow, Inspector?"

"It varies. About four minutes is a rough guide."

"And basically silent . . . I mean the victim can't cry out or do anything much other than struggle increasingly feebly. Perhaps that's your explanation. The dog didn't realise anything was wrong. He's was used to his mistress being ill in bed and to being ministered to by someone, in one way or another."

"Maybe. It's possible."

"But at the moment you have no suspect? And no motive?"

"Oh, we do have a potential motive, sir. Miss Swynford informed us that a valuable diamond brooch that her mother was wearing on the day of the fête is missing. It was worth at least five thousand pounds."

"Do jewel thieves usually murder, Inspector?"

"If they are surprised in the act and panic, they can. Miss Swynford says her mother may have taken the brooch off and put it on her dressing table. It was her habit with jewellery that was likely to be uncomfortable when she was lying down. But she can't swear her mother was wearing it when she went up to rest so it's possible the brooch simply fell off somewhere in the grounds – apparently the clasp was faulty – though so far our men haven't found it." He glanced round the sitting-room. "It isn't here, Inspector, if that's what you're wondering." He smiled a humourless smile. "I didn't think it was, sir. But I wonder if you could tell us your exact movements on the day of the fête? It might help us."

"I arrived at the Manor soon after eleven o'clock, I think. Miss Swynford showed me to the study and then at about midday I took the ten-pound floats round to each stall. I returned to the study and stayed there at the desk until Mrs Beede, the Vicar's wife, came to take over to give me a break. I believe that was around quarter past four. I went to the downstairs cloakroom and then outside. I must have spent about half an hour visiting a few of the stalls, and then I went back inside."

"And Mrs Beede was in the study when you returned?"

"Certainly. The stall takings were there and couldn't be left unattended."

"So there was always somebody in the study, the whole afternoon?"

"That's right."

"And was the door open?"

"It was slightly ajar at first. Then at some point Miss Swynford left it fully open to get some more air into the room. I think that was quite early on in the afternoon. She brought takings from the stalls in to me at intervals so that I could get on with the count-up."

"And from your desk you would have had a clear view of the back hallway."

"I wouldn't say *clear*. The desk was at right angles to the door. But I could see out, yes."

"And do you remember seeing anybody pass in the direction of the main stairs at any time, Colonel?"

## Old Soldiers Never Die

He thought for a moment. "It's difficult . . . I was busy a lot of the time. I remember the odd person went by, and people came into the study – Lady Swynford herself, and Miss Swynford, bringing the stall takings, Mrs Beede, of course, Mrs Grimshaw . . . I really didn't pay much attention. I was busy."

"Anybody who didn't come into the study, though, Colonel? Who just went past?"

He frowned. "I think I saw Miss Butler go by at one point, but I'm not absolutely certain. I only saw a back view. That was later on in the afternoon, I think, after I'd taken a break. She's the committee secretary, of course, and had every right to be around."

"Anybody else?"

He shook his head. "Not that I can remember."

"Well, if you do remember, perhaps you'd let us know, sir. You see, whoever murdered Lady Swynford could hardly have climbed in through the bedroom windows in full view of everyone on the lawn, so they had to enter through the bedroom door. That means they went up one of the two staircases in the house, either the front staircase in the main hall, or the back stairs close to the kitchen wing. The drawing-room French windows were kept shut and locked on that day, and so were all other ground-floor windows, on Lady Swynford's orders. So was the front door and the tradesmen's entrance by the kitchens. But the side entrance was left open for committee members to come and go. Anyone who came in that way and went up the front staircase would have had to pass through the back hall and go by the study, and you might have seen them."

"What about the back stairs?"

"If they used that route, then they didn't need to pass you. The only problem I have with that is that it's a servants' staircase and concealed behind a door. Unless somebody knew the house very well, they wouldn't have known of its existence. You can pass it and think it's just another room. Did you know it existed, sir?"

He found himself bristling and checked it sharply. The man was only doing his job. "No, I didn't. I hardly knew the house at all."

"How long have you been living in Frog End, Colonel?"

"Since early May."

"You're retired, I believe? And a widower?"

"That's right."

"What did you think of Lady Swynford?"

"I only met her three times, Inspector, so I didn't have the opportunity to form much of an opinion."

"Even so, Colonel. You're a pretty good judge of people, I would guess."

He said slowly. "She struck me as a rather affected woman – but as I say, that was only on a brief acquaintance."

"What do you think other people in the village thought of her?"

"I really don't know. I've heard she wasn't particularly popular but of course that doesn't mean that someone would want to murder her, does it? If that happened to all unpopular people you'd have large numbers of corpses on your hands."

Inspector Squibb's mouth stretched into a thin smile. "Very true, sir." He stood up. "We won't take up any more of your time at the present, Colonel, but I may have to trouble you with further questions later on." He reached in his pocket and handed over a card. "Please get in touch with me at once if anything else occurs to you."

"I came to see how you were getting on, Ruth. May I come in for a moment?"

## Old Soldiers Never Die

"Yes, of course."

Tom Harvey followed her into the drawing-room. It was nice of him to call, but all she really wanted was to be left alone. The entire village, it seemed, had written or called or telephoned, and she wasn't up to coping with people yet, with repeating the same things over and over again. 'Yes, it was a great shock. No, the police hadn't the least idea who might have done it. No, she didn't need any food brought round, thank you. No, there was nothing anyone could do, but thank you, all the same.'

He wouldn't sit. "I won't stay long. Just wanted to check up on you."

He had been very kind when he told her about Mama, she remembered; anything but brusque. And when she had broken down, he had let her cry all over his tweedy shoulder and called in every day until she had asked him, please, not to bother any more.

Then there had been the autopsy and the inquest and the police investigation, and the shattering realisation that her mother had been murdered. *Murdered!* A savage and brutal word that she had only read on the front pages of newspapers and never experienced in all its horrible reality.

"I'm all right."

"You don't look it," he said bluntly. "Isn't there anybody who could move in with you for a bit? A cousin, or something? An aunt?"

She shook her head. "No one on my father's side. And my mother cut herself off from her family. I don't want anyone anyway. I'm coping perfectly well."

"Will you stay here at the Manor?"

"Everybody keeps asking me that. I haven't decided what to do yet."

They had all been curious and she had given them all the

same answer. She simply didn't know. The Manor and everything had passed to her to do with as she pleased and, at the moment, she had no idea what did please her. Decisions of any kind were beyond her. She felt alone and vulnerable. And far from being a reassurance, the police had exhausted and frightened her with their endless, searching questions. Inspector Squibb behaved like a Gestapo interrogator, trying to drag information from her when she had already told him everything she knew. Several times over.

She looked up to find Tom Harvey watching her and her mother's words came into her mind: 'Those sort of people always have an eye for the main chance.' And then other words that she'd taken no account of at the time: 'I'm not at all certain he's prescribing me the right pills. They seem to make me feel worse, if anything.' God, she was getting really paranoid. Suspicious of *everybody*.

"The police were here again this morning. Asking more questions."

"Have they made any progress?"

She shrugged. "They think it's possible the motive was robbery. My mother's diamond brooch was missing."

"So I gather. I assume it hasn't been recovered?"

"No." She sank down wearily on the arm of the sofa. "I don't think it was robbery. I think it was someone with a grudge against Mama. Inspector Squibb asked me about that. Who could I think of who might have wanted my mother dead? That's a fairly unpleasant question to be asked."

"Somebody did. And there must have been grudges."

"You don't mince your words either, do you?"

"I mince them up nicely if people can't take it, but you can, Ruth."

"Can I? I used to think I could, but I've been rather wondering lately." She flipped open the silver box on the table nearby and took out a cigarette. "I've taken up smoking again, I'm afraid."

He moved across and lit it for her with the table lighter. She inhaled deeply, looking up at him.

"Aren't you going to read me a doctor's lecture?"

"No. You'll give it up again later on."

"How do you know?"

"You're not the type to need a crutch for long. So, who can you think of who might have had a deep grudge against your mother?"

"Well, Phillipa Rankin, I suppose. Mama had raised her rent and she couldn't afford to pay it so she was going to have to close down her riding school. She came here to ask my mother to reconsider things but mother absolutely refused. I think there was something of a scene. But I've known Phillipa for years, since I was a child, and I couldn't imagine her doing anything like that. It's just not possible."

"Anyone else who might have a reason?"

She hesitated. "Well, there's Jacob, of course. The gardener. You've probably never even seen him. He lives in the old chauffeur's flat. He's a bit of an oddball. Pathologically shy, I suppose you'd say."

"Did he have some kind of grudge, too?"

"My mother fired him. He was only staying till the end of the month. She couldn't stand him . . . said he was always spying on her, but I think she imagined it. He was careful to keep out of her way, that's all. He knew she didn't like him. She didn't want him hired in the first place, but I persuaded her because the garden was in such a mess when I came back. We needed help and he was good. Very good, actually."

"Is he still here?"

"Yes. I told him he could stay on after all . . ." she paused and the words hung on the air. "But he's harmless, Tom. He'd never hurt a fly, I'm certain of that. I've seen him rescuing beetles out of the water butt and freeing birds from the fruit cage. He's *gentle*."

"Did you tell the Inspector about him being fired?"

She shook her head. "No. I didn't want to do that. I didn't want them to upset him. Do you think I should?"

"Yes," he said. "I think you should."

"Let's face it, Hugh," Naomi said breezily. "Any of us in the village could have done it. We *all* disliked her, except for poor old Roger, of course." She sat on the sofa, next to Thursday, wearing a neon-pink tracksuit and white high-top training shoes with pink bits on them to match.

The Colonel got to his feet. "The other half?"

"Rather! Just a splash of water."

He refilled their glasses from the whisky decanter and sat down again.

"Cheers."

She tipped her glass. "Bottoms up. Down the hatch."

"You say everyone disliked Lady Swynford, but some more than others, who, for example?"

"Me, for starters. She broke my sister's heart. Took away her happiness and the life she would have had with Alan. I never forgave her for that. I'd cheerfully have done her in."

He smiled. "Well, assuming you didn't, who else might have been tempted?"

"Marjorie Cuthbertson – for the way she was carrying on with Roger?"

"A bit drastic, surely? It was bound to end sooner or later, when Lady Swynford got tired of it."

"Roger, then? Slighted love? Hell hath no fury like an old man scorned who fancies he's still a young Lothario."

## Old Soldiers Never Die

He thought of the Major blundering past him out of the Manor on the day of the fête. Surely not him?

"And Phillipa Rankin." Naomi went on, after taking another glug at her glass. "Ursula had upped her rent so much she was going to have to close down. That won't happen now with Ruth, you can bet your bottom dollar."

"Ruth inherits everything?"

"So one gathers. The Manor, the money, the lot. The house was entailed, anyway. The baronetcy died out with Alan, of course. There were no male relatives."

"What about the missing brooch and the robbery theory? That's perfectly possible, surely. There were strangers around that day. Potential thieves."

Naomi dismissed that airily. "Don't believe a word of it. Whoever topped Ursula pinched the brooch to make it *look* like robbery. To divert suspicion. It's been chucked in the village pond, or something."

The phone went and he excused himself to answer. It was Susan about the weekend. They would be coming on Friday afternoon, not Saturday morning. Marcus had got the day off so that they could make it a long weekend with him.

"Bad news?" Naomi asked.

"Just my daughter-in-law. They're coming this Friday."

"Have you done a dummy run with those recipes?"

"I cooked some new potatoes, or rather undercooked them. And I burnt a pork chop. I can manage frozen peas."

"You've got to do better than that, Hugh. Practice makes perfect."

"There's the cake I won at the fête."

"You sound like Marie Antoinette. They can't eat that all weekend. We'd better work out the meals and make a shopping list for you. Stick to simple things, like I said. Which reminds me . . ." she groped in the pocket of her tracksuit and produced a screwed-up bit of paper "...another easy one for you. Rhubarb crumble. Nothing to it." To his amazement, when he looked at the recipe he saw that she had spelt everything right.

Damned tricky business. He'd never been in such a tight spot in all his life. What the hell was he going to do? God, he needed another drink, a stiff top-up before Marjorie came into the room. He could hear her crashing about in the kitchen down the corridor. He wouldn't be able to eat whatever it was she was concocting in there – the stomach couldn't face it tonight. Well, that wouldn't be anything new. The old girl wasn't the best cook in the world. It was never exactly Gourmet Night at Shangri-La. Not her fault, of course. They'd always been used to servants abroad to do the bloody cooking and everything else.

The Major shut the living room door quietly and tiptoed across to the cocktail cabinet. The confounded thing played a tune when you opened it and Marjorie had ears like a bat. He opened and shut the lid quickly, cutting off the tinkling notes of 'Drink to me only with thine eyes' in mid-bar, and poured a large tot from the whisky bottle before he returned it equally fast. He'd got that little manoeuvre down to a fine art. The cabinet had been a retirement present from the regiment and he still wasn't sure that it hadn't been some kind of joke at his expense.

He took a gulp and hung on to the back of an armchair, trying to steady himself. No point getting into a muck sweat. He'd got to stay calm or the old girl would smell a rat. Now *that* was a saying that made sense. They'd had a dead rat under the floorboards in their quarters once, he couldn't remember where. Stank the place out and had gone on smelling for weeks after it had been carted off. Yes, Marjorie would smell a rat if he didn't get a grip on himself. Or smell the whisky, more likely, and know he'd drunk too much. Even more than usual, it had to be said. 'What's the matter, Roger?' she'd ask with that gimlet look in her eye. It was never any good not answering. 'Cat got your tongue?' she'd say next. Damned silly – they hadn't even got a cat, but one thing was for sure if they had one it would be out of the bag and among the pigeons. No doubt about it. Never any use beating about the bush with the old girl once she'd got a bee in her bonnet.

For a moment he considered telling her. Coming straight out with it. Making a clean breast of things. But only for a moment. The Major sighed and took another swallow. Out of the question, of course. Out of the question.

Miss Butler stood staring out of her sitting-room window. It was a beautiful summer evening and there was going to be a glorious sunset by the look of the sky. A part of her mind registered that fact because she had always liked sunsets, and the other part grappled with the nightmare. How could she have done it? What evil demon had possessed her? And how was she going to live with what she had done? How could she find the strength to go on?

In anguish, she turned her eyes to the photograph on the bureau, seeking comfort, but her father gazed at her in contempt. There was no help there. She bowed her head and covered her face with her hands.

# Eleven

"Hasn't Eric grown, Father?"
"My goodness, yes."
The Colonel stared down at his grandson who had just emerged sulkily from the back of the estate car, dragging a toy rabbit by the ear.

"He's four now, you now."

"Yes, of course," God, he must have forgotten the child's birthday; there had been a definite reproach in Susan's voice. "Hallo there, Eric."

He had been unable to warm to the blotchy-faced, squalling infant on their first acquaintance soon after his birth, and now that Eric had grown into a small boy he still felt guiltily unenthusiastic. The boy looked so like Susan. There was absolutely nothing of Marcus in him, that he could see. He had his mother's gooseberry eyes and pale skin and her wispy hair. And he would probably inherit her temperament, too; perhaps even her way of speaking.

His daughter-in-law's voice grated on his ears again.

"Say hello to Grandfather, then, Eric."

Eric ignored them both. His looked around him, unimpressed, and clutched the rabbit closer. "I feel sick."

Marcus, burdened with suitcases and nursery impedimenta, seemed tired and harrassed. It had been a ghastly drive down, he said. There'd been a long hold up on the M5 when he'd thought the car was going to overheat and seize up, and Eric had felt sick most of the way.

The Colonel showed them into the cottage and Eric demonstrated his feelings by vomiting instantly onto the sitting-room room carpet. When that had been cleared up, with Susan rushing about with bowls of disinfectant, there was a drama over the sleeping arrangements. Eric refused to sleep on his own and his wails upstairs turned to hysterical screams.

"He's highly strung, you see," Susan explained later when he had been induced to lie down with the rabbit and had, apparently, fallen asleep. She had changed into something flowery with a frill round the neck which should have made her look prettier but, in fact, had the opposite effect. "The psychologist says it's important recognise that and make allowances. Marcus will sleep in the single room tonight and Eric can come in with me."

"You've taken him to a psychologist?"

"Oh, yes. We were afraid that he was hyperactive at one point."

Hyperspoilt more probably the Colonel thought privately, remembering the constant temper tantrums, but he reserved his judgement. Who was he to know? Child psychology was a closed book to him.

He said; "I've done a shepherd's pie for supper. Will that be all right?"

"Oh, Eric wouldn't touch that, I'm afraid. He's a very difficult eater. I've brought his in tins." Susan was looking wary. "Did you make it yourself?"

He had spent yesterday doing so. Chopping onions and frying mince and mashing potatoes and the result this time had been a surprising improvement on the last effort. When he had tasted a cautious spoonful it hadn't seemed too bad.

"As a matter of fact I did." He opened the fridge door to

## Old Soldiers Never Die

show her the pie sitting there in all its glory, ready to be reheated. She peered in at it suspiciously. "You needn't have troubled, Father. I brought a home-cooked casserole with us. I only have to pop it in the oven."

He sighed inwardly. All that trouble... Oh, well, may be it would keep and he and Thursday could live on it during the week. More probably, he, since Thursday's approval was always in the balance.

"You ought to go to evening classes in cookery, Father." Susan suggested, evidently unimpressed by her look into the fridge.

"I have a kind neighbour who's giving me hints."

"Oh? A lady?"

"A widow," he said and observed her instantly alert glance with amusement. "She comes round quite often."

"You have to be careful, you know, Father."

"Careful?"

"Well, you know widows ... and you're ... well, you're ..."

"A widower?" he said innocently.

"Well, yes."

He smiled at her; it wasn't fair to go on teasing her. "I know what you're driving at, my dear, but I can assure you that I'm in no danger from my neighbour. Or she from me," he added as an afterthought and watched the blush rising like the morning sun from under the frill round Susan's neck.

She changed the subject hurriedly, producing a package wrapped in gift paper.

"We've brought you a little present, Father."

He was touched, if apprehensive. The wrapping paper had posies of flowers all over it and there was a knot of shiny green ribbon stuck in one corner. He undid it all and found a photograph of Eric, mounted in a red velvet frame. It had been taken against a vivid blue background and the colours were technicolour-crude. Eric was scowling at the camera.

"We thought you ought to have one, Father. The photographer came to the play school and took all the children. You know Eric goes to playgroup two mornings a week, don't you?"

He was ashamed to say that he didn't. Or if he did, he had forgotten. And he was also ashamed of his lack of interest in his grandson. Laura would have known all those sort of things about him, and would never have forgotten his birthday. He thanked Susan and placed the photograph prominently on the table in the sitting-room.

In the evening when the casserole was heating in the oven and they were having a drink, Susan returned to the attack.

"You really should try an evening class, Father. It would get you out of the house."

What sort, he wondered grimly? How to make raffia baskets? Or dried flower arrangements like Mrs Townsend? Susan had admired the hoop-la trophy where he had parked it on a kitchen shelf. Woodwork, perhaps? Japanese origami?

"I've taken up German," she informed him earnestly, sipping her sherry. "Haven't I, Marcus? You could try a language, Father. German's rather difficult, though, so I should do an easier language, if I were you. It's got different cases, you see, and awfully long words. I don't know why they have to have them so long."

As a matter of fact he was pretty fluent in German. The army had sent him on a course and he'd made good use of it when they had been stationed over there. He didn't say so, though.

"It's certainly an idea. I'll think about it."

Fortunately the weather was fine on Saturday and they were able to go for a walk in the afternoon. The morning had

## Old Soldiers Never Die

passed fairly quietly, except for Thursday spitting at Eric and scratching his arm. The Colonel deeply suspected the child of pulling the cat's tail first. There had been ear-splitting howls and then more howls as Susan applied copious amounts of TCP. Thursday had been banished to the garden, tail thrashing furiously. "He's not a very nice cat, is he?" Susan had said. "I wonder why you keep him?" He had often wondered the same thing himself.

For lunch they finished up Susan's casserole from the night before, while Eric created havoc over his baked beans. For tea he produced the 'Guess the Weight' cake and Eric who had demanded to be given the big sugar rose in the centre, spat the angelica leaves out onto the table. Later on, when the bathtime and bedtime screams from upstairs had finally died away into blessed silence, the Colonel announced firmly that he was going to cook dinner: steak, micro-baked potatoes and salad.

"*Steak!*" Susan reproved, as though he had proposed caviar. "Marcus and I never have steak. It's much too expensive."

He succeeded in keeping her out of the kitchen and in making a reasonable job of the meal. Naomi had made up salad dressing in a screw-top jar, so it was a simple question of putting tomatoes and lettuce in a bowl, the potatoes in the microwave oven, and of frying the steak so that it was neither over-cooked nor raw. Not totally beyond him, as it proved. And even Naomi's 'choclate moose' recipe, about which he had had grave doubts, turned out rather well.

To his politely concealed relief, Susan went to bed early and he had the chance of some time alone with Marcus. His son had seemed preoccupied and depressed for most of the weekend and he wondered exactly what was troubling him. When he had poured them both a nightcap whisky, he asked him straight out. Marcus, after a glance at the door to make sure it was closed, gave him an equally straight answer.

"I've been sacked from the firm, Dad. Booted out. Made redundant is the euphemism they use these days, but it comes down to the same thing. As of the end of this month I don't have a job." He was trying to make light of it, but failing.

"I'm so sorry . . ." The Colonel searched quickly for words of comfort and encouragement. "It seems to be happening to a great many good people these days. You'll find another job soon enough."

"I certainly hope so. I wrote off to other firms as soon as they told me. So far, no luck."

"You're a young man with good experience in business, Marcus," he said, thinking of the stack of negative replies he'd received to his own applications. "You've got plenty to offer."

"I suppose so."

"Susan hasn't mentioned it."

"She doesn't know. I haven't told her yet. Couldn't face it. Cowardly of me, I know. She'll have to know sooner or later, of course. I'm just not sure how badly she'll take it. And it will probably mean moving house."

"I'm sure she'll cope perfectly well. Women do. Remember your mother."

Marcus nodded. "Of course, you were always moving, weren't you? We were always coming back to different homes in the holidays. Mum didn't seem to mind, did she?"

If she had, he thought, Laura had never complained. But she'd always talked of how they'd settle down in one place, one day.

"There's Eric to think about, too," Marcus went on. "He's just started at his playschool."

"Children are pretty adaptable, surely, especially at that age. I shouldn't worry about that."

## Old Soldiers Never Die

"Actually, it's Susan I'm much more worried about. She's just got the house how she likes it."

Uncharitable memories of bleak parquet, Dralon and teak floated into the Colonel's mind. He banished them sternly.

"She'll cope," he repeated, but with more optimism than he really felt. He had a feeling that Susan might throw a fit, and Marcus's reluctance to tell her boded ill. If Laura were here she would have known exactly what to do and say. He felt almost as inadequate with his son as he felt with his grandson.

"If there's anything I can do, Marcus . . . financially, or in any way at all, just let me know. You can count on me for any help you need."

On Sunday it poured with rain. To please Susan they went to church and Eric squirmed and grizzled all the way through the service. Ruth Swynford was alone in the front pew. Brave of her, he thought, to face the inquisitive stares. Prayers were said by the Vicar for Lady Swynford's soul and her eternal rest, and he wondered how many of the congregation were joining in with any sincerity. The 'Amen' certainly sounded very faint. He hadn't mentioned the murder to Susan or Marcus. Susan, he felt sure, would have strongly disapproved of him living where something like that could happen and would have started telling him yet again about how much better it would be if he were near them. He had gallantly ceded the kitchen to her for the lunch. Eric rejected any of the roast chicken and dropped his peas one by one onto the carpet.

After tea the Colonel waved them away with something close to relief, though he disguised it well, standing at the cottage gateway and waving and smiling until they were out of sight. Eric had refused to say goodbye, just as he had refused to say hello. Perhaps children, the same as animals, sensed if they were not much liked, in which case he could hardly blame him any more than he had been able to blame him for spitting out the angelica leaves.

Dear Friends,
    We are all united in our shock and sorrow at the tragic death of Lady Swynford who was a part of all our lives for so many years. She was a gracious patron and benefactress who held the interests of our beautiful village close to her heart. We extend our deepest sympathy to her daughter, Ruth, in her great loss and assure her of our constant prayers and support . . .

The Vicar paused and read carefully through what he had just written. Except for the last part, it was all lies, of course. He, for one, could not be sorry about Lady Swynford's passing and this month's magazine letter to his parishioners was nothing less than shocking hypocrisy. Nobody mourned, except her daughter, as far as he could tell, and the only interest Lady Swynford had held close to her heart was her own. Usually he enjoyed writing his monthly message, but this one troubled him deeply. He should have been writing of the glorious fruits of summer, perhaps with a salutary reference to those parts of the world where there was terrible famine, in stark contrast to this country's bounty. And it was time to remind his parishioners of the blessing of the holiday season just ahead when there would time for refreshment and renewal of both the body and the spirit . . . a time for quiet meditation and thankfulness.

The Lord is my Shepherd: therefore can I lack nothing. He shall feed me in a green pasture: and lead me forth beside the waters of comfort . . .

\* \* \*

## Old Soldiers Never Die

The study door opened and Jean wheeled herself in.

"Still working, William?"

"It's a difficult letter to write this month," he told her. "I don't quite know what to put."

"Finish it later," she advised. The chair hummed its way over to the corner cupboard. "A drink is what you need. It'll do you good."

She took out the bottle of whisky that he had won at the fête and poured some into a glass and then some sherry for herself. He demurred as she held his glass out to him.

"Do you think –?"

"I certainly do."

"But whisky . . ."

"You won it, William. And you deserve it. Besides, it's a celebration."

"A celebration?"

"We're toasting your new patron," she said calmly. "That's quite in order." She raised her glass. "To Ruth. God bless her."

"God bless her," he echoed fervently, and drank.

"Sorry to trouble you again, Colonel." Inspector Squibb didn't look or sound in the least sorry. "Just a couple more questions, if you don't mind."

He was alone this time and without the civilising presence of his sergeant. He didn't bother with sitting down.

"You mentioned that Miss Swynford brought the takings in to you in the study at intervals throughout the afternoon of the fête, sir?"

"That's so."

"Was there any gap in this procedure? Any longer period between these deliveries?"

He remembered Naomi coming in herself with her overflowing plastic bowl. "It's rather hard to say, Inspector. Miss Swynford didn't bring the takings at absolutely regular intervals. I imagine she waited until a stall had amassed a reasonable amount. There was no definite pattern or timing."

"I see. And when she came to tell you that something was wrong with her mother, what were her exact words?"

He frowned. "I believe she said, 'It's my mother. I think she's dead.' Something like that."

"Did she seem very distressed?"

"Well, naturally she did, Inspector. It must have been a great shock. She asked me to try to find Dr Harvey, which I did."

"She knew he was there, then? At the fête?"

"Obviously. Or guessed that he would be. I think most of the village attended."

"And you left Miss Swynford in the study while you fetched the doctor?"

"That's right."

"And you and Dr Harvey went upstairs to Lady Swynford's bedroom together, sir?"

"That's correct."

"And at that point Lady Swynford was already dead?"

"I'm not a doctor, Inspector, but she certainly looked it. Surely Dr Harvey must have already testified to that."

"I just wanted to be quite clear about some things. Did you leave the room while Dr Harvey was examining Lady Swynford?"

"No. I stayed. I thought I might be needed, for one reason or another."

The Inspector paused for a moment, as though digesting these answers. "Were you aware, Colonel, that Miss Swynford and Dr Harvey had been meeting socially?"

"No."

## Old Soldiers Never Die

"They were seen having dinner together recently. Somebody happened to spot them."

"I can't quite see where all this is leading, Inspector."

"Nowhere particular, sir. As yet. It's just that in a murder case, we tend to look for our suspects among the victim's family, before anywhere else. You'd be surprised how often it turns out to be a close relative who's responsible."

He said impatiently, "What possible reason could Miss Swynford have for murdering her mother – if that's what you're implying? The idea is quite absurd."

"Money. Freedom. Hatred. Resentment. Those are all quite common motives, Colonel."

"Miss Swynford came home to care for her mother, Inspector. Hardly the act of a potential murderess. And to suggest that Dr Harvey might be involved is slanderous –"

"I didn't say he was, sir. I merely asked if you knew they were socially acquainted."

He's dirt-digging, the Colonel thought angrily. Sniffing around to see what he can find. Listening to what people will say. Raking up all the local gossip. He's sharp and sleek – like a ferret – poking his nose into every dark crevice and corner.

"I should have thought the missing brooch was a better line of inquiry, Inspector. Have you had any luck recovering it yet?"

"No. Frankly, I didn't expect to. Wherever it is, it's well hidden, for the time being. Lady Swynford had quite a collection of valuable jewellery. Her late husband was evidently a very generous man. Did you know that she was a dancer before she met him?"

"Was she?" he said shortly. "Isn't that rather irrelevant?"

"Not necessarily. We did a little investigating. She was born in Streatham and went on the stage at sixteen as a dancer. She did some kind of nightclub solo act later on dancing with seven veils. Rather interesting, I thought."

"I fail to see why. It must have been a very long time ago."

"But then you're not investigating this murder, Colonel, so you wouldn't. To me, each and every piece of information is a piece of the whole puzzle that I'm trying to solve."

The Inspector moved towards the sitting-room door and then paused. "By the way, we interviewed Miss Butler. She confirmed that it *was* her you saw passing the study. Apparently she had come into the house in search of the downstairs toilet. There was a long queue at the Portaloos outside and she didn't want to wait – I think it embarrassed her to have to stand there, in public."

The Colonel watched a smirk pass over Squibb's face. Poor Miss Butler, trying to explain her predicament. He was sorry he had ever mentioned seeing her. "Well, if that's all, Inspector, I'll see you out." He wanted the man gone before he lost his temper. The whole thing was distasteful to him.

At the sitting-room door, Squibb paused again. "I understand you gave the gardener at the Manor some work here recently, sir?"

'He helped me with a clearing job, on a casual basis."

"Did he do it well?"

"Very. He's an excellent worker."

"You didn't find him a bit peculiar?"

"He's extremely shy and not very good with people, if that's what you mean."

"As a matter of fact, he's rather more than that. He was a patient for several years at a mental hospital – some kind of severe personality hang-up. That's where he learned to garden – as therapy. Before that he was in a children's home. His mother left him on the doorstep, apparently, in a cardboard box. They called him Jacob because the box had contained

*Old Soldiers Never Die*

Jacob's Cream Crackers." Another faint smirk. "Rather appropriate."

"One of your puzzle pieces, Inspector?" the Colonel asked coldly. The Inspector's warped idea of humour did not appeal to him.

"It could well be, sir. You see, Miss Swynford has informed us that her mother fired Jacob shortly before she was murdered. He was to go at the end of the month. Now, he won't have to."

The Colonel shut the front door after the Inspector and went back into the sitting-room. As an antidote to his irritation, he put on one of his Gilbert and Sullivan records and sat down to listen to *The Mikado*.

> A wand'ring minstrel I –
> A thing of shreds and patches.
> Of ballads songs and snatches,
> And dreamy lullaby!

He let the familiar music wash over him soothingly and beat time with his hand on the chair arm as he listened.

> My catalogue is long
> For every passion ranging.
> And to your humours changing,
> I tune my soulful song . . .

For once it didn't quite work. His beat slowed gradually and he started to think, rather than listen.

It was intriguing to speculate who had murdered Lady Swynford. Who *was* it who had hated her so much? Or needed her dead? And why?

Naomi had been right. There were a number of people who

might qualify, for varying reasons. He went over the possibilities in his mind, considering them, and he thought of one or two that Naomi hadn't mentioned. It was all speculation, of course. Shots in the dark. Hunches. Nothing more than that. But someone in the village had done it, he was certain of that. The diamond brooch was a red herring. One of them had planned and executed the murder of Ursula Swynford and it would be an interesting exercise to see if he could solve the Inspector's grim little puzzle before he did.

As some day it may happen that a victim must be found,
I've got a little list – I've got a little list . . .

The phone rang and he got up to answer it. It was Marcus.

"Hold on a minute, old chap. I'll turn the record player down." He picked up the receiver again. "How are things?"

"I told Susan," his son said baldly. "She thinks it's all my fault. That I must have done something wrong at work. I tried to explain, but she doesn't seem to understand anything about the recession. She got in a frightful state about it all."

"Give her time, Marcus. She'll get used to it and realise that it isn't the end of the world, by any means."

"Well, she's getting used to it at her mother's. She packed a suitcase and took Eric off there with her. Said she wanted to get away."

She could take the fair weather, but not the foul, the Colonel thought, depressed. His gut feeling had been right. "Have you had any news from those firms you wrote to?"

"A couple of standard replies – they haven't got anything but they'll keep my letter on file. It's just a polite way of saying they're not interested and never will be."

"Keep at it, Marcus," he said firmly. "Don't let it get you

*Old Soldiers Never Die*

down. Something will turn up soon. When does Susan come back?"

"No idea. Maybe never. She wouldn't say. Her mother'll probably talk her into staying there permanently."

He searched through his memories of the wedding day and came up with an older edition of Susan, also in something frilly, fussing protectively round her daughter. "I'd go and fetch her, if I were you. Her place is with you. You ought to get through this together."

"To tell you the truth, Dad, I'm not sure if I want her back – ever."

Marcus sounded miserable, angry, and bitter, all rolled into one. It was even worse than he had feared. Laura, he asked himself, where are you? I need you to help sort this thing out?

# Twelve

"I don't much care for that Squabb chap."

"Inspector Squibb?"

"Squabb, Squibb, whatever he is. He tried to give me the third degree." Naomi's purple-clad chest swelled with indignation. "I sent him off with a flea in his ear."

The Colonel smiled. "I'd like to have been there."

"Grilled me about where was I when the lights went out, so to speak . . . as though we were playing a game of Murder. Had I stayed at my stall all afternoon? Well, I told him *he* might have an everlasting bladder but I didn't. Then he had the nerve to trot out all that old history about Alan and Jess, and ask had I been very fond of my sister . . . I could see his drift, so I cut it short. Told him I'd got an excellent reason for bumping off Ursula but why should I wait till now when I've had nearly forty years to do it at my leisure. What's that you're trying to plant?"

"Something called *Acanthus spinosus*. I got it at a garden centre. Am I doing it right?"

"Except that it's in the wrong place. You want to put it at the back of the border. It'll grow about four feet tall."

"What do you suggest for the front here, then?"

"Something pretty that'll spill over. Alchemilla. Or maybe gypsophila. I'll write them down for you, if you like."

"Thanks, Naomi." The Colonel got up off his knees and

dusted them down. "What else did Inspector Squibb ask you?"

"What I could remember seeing. Where everyone was. What they were doing. I told you, it was like playing a game of Murder."

"What *could* you remember?"

She cocked her head on one side. "Why the interest?"

"I'm just rather curious. Somebody managed to get into the house and up to Lady Swynford's bedroom to kill her during the afternoon and they did it between about three fifteen when she went up to rest and six o'clock when she was found dead. I wondered what you'd noticed."

"Well now, let me see. I didn't bother much when that Squibb man asked me, but I'll exercise the brain-box for *you*, Hugh. I was pretty busy, though."

"Well, let's start at the beginning, from when the gates opened and Lady Swynford made her speech."

Naomi snorted. "Typical Ursula, queening it over the peasants. I was rushed off my feet for all the first part – people buying all those hideous petunias. Freda Butler gave me a hand for a bit – she was sort of wandering around, helping out, I think. Ruth came round to get the first lot of takings, and I remember seeing Ursula swanning around, doing her gracious Lady of the Manor act, taking turns round the stalls, talking to people. I think she must have upset Roger a bit because I noticed him looking like a whipped puppy after she'd left the bottle stall. Poor old Roger. I say, Hugh, you don't seriously think . . . I was only joking about him before, you know. Anyway, he couldn't have, he was stuck at his stall all afternoon."

"Was he?"

Naomi frowned. "Come to think of it, no. Marjorie took over later on, for a while, sometime around four, I think. I noticed her there when I came in to bring the takings to you myself. I don't know where Ruth had got to, but Freda had come by so I grabbed her to hold the fort for me for five minutes."

It must have been about a quarter to five when he had passed the Major hurrying out of the house, the Colonel reckoned, so he had been at large for quite some time.

"What else can you remember?"

Naomi screwed up her eyes. "Not much. I was frightfully busy. Marjorie Cuthbertson bought a jolly nice *Iris orchroleuca* that I rather wished I'd kept for myself. She'll probably kill it. Dr Harvey came up at one point, but he didn't buy anything – I don't think he's got time for gardening. He'd just won a toy elephant at the hoop-la. I remember laughing about it and he said he'd picked it out for the children's box in the surgery. The Vicar bought a potentilla for Jean – but that was later on because I remember I'd nearly run out of wrapping stuff and he found some more newspaper under the table. 'Gibson's Scarlet' – horrible colour so I shouldn't think she'll like it, though she won't let on, of course. Sorry, none of that's any help, is it? Just bits and pieces."

"It might be," he said. "If I put them all together."

Alison phoned that evening.

"I hear Susan's gone running home to Mummy. Marcus called me. He's pretty cut up, isn't he? I didn't say so, but personally I hope she stays there, Dad. I think he'd be a lot better off without her."

The same ignoble thought had occurred to the Colonel more than once in the past few days, but he had managed to suppress it. At one point he had been on the verge of getting into the Riley and driving up to Essex where Susan's parents lived. Then he had heard Laura speaking as clearly as though she were in the room with him. 'Don't interfere, Hugh. You might make matters worse. It's up to Marcus and Susan to work it out for themselves.'

"It's only temporary," he said. "It happens in marriages."

"Not with you and Mum. Not like that. Mum would never have gone off when you most needed her. I think Susan's absolutely pathetic."

They were chalk and cheese, Alison and Susan, of course, which is why they had never got on. But she was quite right about her mother.

On the next day, the Colonel went back to the garden centre and wandered up and down the long rows of benches. By the alpines he encountered Ruth Swynford, carrying a plant tucked under her arm.

"Hello, Colonel," she said, in answer to his greeting. She looked pale and strained, he thought, but she smiled at him quite cheerfully. "I'm surprised you didn't hide behind a rose bush, or something."

"Why should I do that?"

"People keep avoiding me. Everyone was terribly nice at first but now suddenly they give me a wide berth. I suppose it's because they don't know what to say any more. I'm beginning to know how lepers must have felt."

"It's a common experience in bereavement, I'm afraid."

"Of course, I'd forgotten you would know . . ."

They moved on down the row. Arabis, Santolina, Saxifraga, he read. Armeria, Cerastium . . . He stopped to consult the piece of paper Naomi had given him.

"I'm looking for something called alchemilla or, failing that, gypsophila," he said. "I don't suppose you can help me?"

"You're in the wrong section, I'm afraid." She pointed to a

far corner. They'll be over there. I'll come with you, if you like."

"That would be very kind."

"I hear Inspector Squibb has been to see you, Colonel." she said as they walked on. "Did you find him as unpleasant as I did?"

"Extremely so."

"He seems to think I may have had something to do with my mother's death. Apparently murder is often a family affair, so he informed me. He was fairly offensive about it all. Then he suddenly switched the interrogation spotlight onto poor Jacob and put him through pretty good hell. I kept telling him that he never goes *near* the house and that he's perfectly harmless. Of course Jacob was hopeless at answering questions . . . about where he was and so on."

"Where *was* he? Do you know?"

"Not exactly. Once the gates opened and people started coming in he'd have pushed off and hidden himself away somewhere. In the potting shed, probably. Actually, I saw him near there in the kitchen gardens at one point, and I told the Inspector so."

"The kitchen gardens?" he said surprised, wondering what she had been doing there in the middle of the fete. He glanced at her and saw she had blushed.

"I didn't tell the Inspector this, but I was with a friend. An ex-lover, as a matter of fact, to be frank with you, Colonel, and I know you won't repeat this. He'd turned up with his wife at the fête – all quite by chance. He wanted to talk and I arranged to meet him there at quarter to four. So, I know Jacob was there at that time. And, in any case, I don't see how he could possibly have got in and out of the house without being seen. He's not exactly unnoticeable."

"He lives in a flat in the old stables, doesn't he? I imagine the police have searched his rooms?"

"Searched is an understatement, Colonel. They tore the place apart looking for my mother's brooch mainly, I suppose. They didn't find a thing, and the funny part is that it turned up anyway this morning."

"Turned up?"

"In the mail. It was sent back in one of those padded envelopes, addressed to me in block letters, with a Dorchester post mark. I told the Inspector, of course, and handed it over. They've taken it all away to test for fingerprints and things, I suppose."

They had reached the section that she had indicated, marked by a large notice: PERENNIALS.

"What was it you were looking for, Colonel? I've forgotten what you said?"

He held out his bit of paper. "Naomi suggested these."

Ruth Swynford looked and laughed. "She's a terrible speller, isn't she? But she always gives good advice, and her own plants are wonderful."

"I remember you bought one at the fête."

"The dicentra? I went and left it in the study, didn't I? Was it you who put it in the sink for me and watered it? I wondered when I found it there eventually."

He shook his head. "I gave it to your mother. It seemed rather dry and drooping."

She smiled at him. "You'll make a good gardener, Colonel. You've a feeling for plants."

"Have I?"

"Oh yes. And for people, too, I'd say." She turned to the plants displayed on the bench. "Look, here's a fairly decent alchemilla. I think Naomi would approve."

He took the plant, thanking her. It was a pretty thing, he thought, with its tiny pale green flowers and crinkly leaves.

"You have to be careful when you choose here," she told him. "The quality varies. I've had some dismal failures. Actually, I've often thought I'd like to start up a place of my own one day."

"Why don't you?"

She shook her head, smiling. "I can't think about it now. I can't seem to think about anything except what happened to my mother and wanting them to find out whoever did it. Do you think we'll ever know?"

"Oh yes," he promised her rashly. "We will. Miss Swynford, can you think of anything your mother said to you on the day of the fête that might provide some clue. What did she say to you before she went up to rest, for instance."

"Well, she asked me about Ralph and said how secretive I'd been about my life in London. Then she said something else about how surprising it was that people could keep secrets for years, but that she wasn't referring to me. I can't remember her exact words, but I thought she was actually thinking of the secret she'd kept about herself – about working in a nightclub. But, of course, she may have been meaning something quite different."

"She didn't give you any kind of clue?"

"I'm afraid not. I wish I'd paid more attention. Do you think it might have had something to do with her death, Colonel?"

"It might have," he said. "Just possibly."

Frog End Vicarage was a modern red-brick bungalow built close to others like it at one end of the village, not far from Journey's End of the Colonel's previous acquaintance. The former Vicarage, he knew, was the Georgian stone house, close to the church which had long since been sold to a private owner. Walking up the macadam driveway to the front door, he wondered if Vicars minded being turfed out of lovely old Vicarages and put into modern places with so little charm. He pressed the bell that ding-donged in response and waited, rehearsing his excuse for calling. After a while he heard the hum of the electric wheelchair somewhere inside and glimpsed the amorphous shape of it and Mrs Beede just beyond the reeded glass panels. She opened the door to him smiling.

"Hello, Colonel. How nice to see you. Will you come in?"

He stepped into a small, carpeted hallway and followed her down a passage into the living room. It was light and pleasant, with a large picture window and a sliding glass door onto the back garden. The furniture was Swedish modern. She swivelled the wheelchair to face him and, again, he was struck by how well she manoeuvered it, as smoothly as if it were a part of herself. Practice, he supposed, made perfect, as Naomi would say.

"William's not in at the moment, I'm afraid, he's gone to choir practice. I expect you came to see him?"

He had come to see either of them, both if possible, and trotted out his excuse.

"I came to offer my services in the churchyard. Your husband mentioned that help was needed mowing the grass, and so on."

"How very kind of you, Colonel. I'm sure William will be glad of any time you can spare. It's always a problem to keep it in good order. And so important William always feels. He says we must take care of the dead in the parish as well as the living. And he's right, don't you agree?"

"Certainly."

"And of course the church itself is so beautiful and so worth preserving at all costs."

"I hope the proceeds from the fête will be a help."

"Oh, yes. Though I'm sure we all feel that day was rather overshadowed by Lady Swynford's death."

## Old Soldiers Never Die

He murmured something appropriate. "The police don't seem to be any nearer to finding the murderer."

"So it seems." She gave him a questioning look. "An Inspector called here to interview William and me. I'm afraid we weren't able to be much help. I don't remember noticing anything unusual or suspicious at the fête, and nor does William."

"I wondered if perhaps you noticed anything, or anybody in the house while you were there, holding the fort for me?"

"I don't think so. William helped me up over the outside step, at the side entrance that leads into the back hall, you know, and then he went off and I came whizzing straight round to the study to find you. When you left I stayed there until you got back. I didn't see anybody else except for you."

"Nobody passed the open door of the study? Nobody at all?"

"The Inspector asked me the same. I don't remember noticing anybody, but then, of course, I had my back turned to it. And I was busy re-counting the plant stall takings for you. I lost my place once and had to start all over again, so it took a while. I really wasn't paying attention to anything else."

She had made the total exactly the same as him, he remembered. He also remembered that her wheelchair had, indeed, been at the front of the desk, turned away from the door.

"I hear the missing brooch was returned," she went on, "which makes it even more mysterious. Do you have any theories, Colonel?"

"None at the moment."

"I hope for poor Ruth's sake that whoever killed her mother will be brought to justice."

"So do I."

"Can I offer you a drink, Colonel. We actually have some whisky – the bottle that William won at the fête."

"No, thank you. I won't keep you."

"You must come and look at my garden before you go. I'm very proud of it. William made special height flowerbeds for me, you know. He adapted everything in the house, too, all the switches and the work-top levels in the kitchen, people don't realise how difficult it is to manage from a wheelchair otherwise. And he made all these ramps so I can get around everywhere when I'm on my own. He's wonderful at DIY." She led the way out into the garden, powering the chair easily over the ramped sill.

It was much smaller than his own at Pond Cottage – the sort of dull, square plot that he would have had at Journey's End – but Jean Beede had succeeded in transforming it into something very charming. He admired roses in full bloom, a variety of shrubs and climbers and something that looked like a honeysuckle rambling happily along the fence. The flower beds, he saw, had been raised on wooden frames to a couple of feet or more off the ground and the effect of plants spilling over and trailing freely was exceedingly attractive.

"My Hanging Gardens of Babylon," Jean Beede said, handwheeling herself slowly along. "Are you a gardener, Colonel?"

"I'm afraid not. But I'm a pupil of Naomi Grimshaw. She's trying to teach me the rudiments."

"She's a wonderful gardener, isn't she? She's given me all sorts of nice cuttings. It's something you can get very hooked on, you know. I didn't have a clue either until we came here. There was nothing out here but builders' rubble, then, and it was so depressing that something had to be done. It's very therapeutic, I find. When I'm out here, working away, I forget about all the things I want to forget about."

Naomi, of course, had said much the same thing, he remembered. He walked along a flower bed beside the wheelchair. And like Naomi, Jean Beede seemed to favour soft, natural colours blending with different foliages – dark green, pale green, silvery, variagated. He liked the look of it very much and hoped his efforts would turn out half as well. He watched her pulling out a stray weed and snapping off an over-long shoot. In spite of her crippled state, there seemed to be reasonable strength in her hands and arms.

"William bought me a potentilla from Naomi's stall at the fête, He meant so well, poor William, but he'd forgotten how I don't much like potentillas and I simply *hate* reds like that. Actually I hate reds of any kind. I've planted it out of sight in a corner, poor thing. I hope plants don't have feelings."

"I think Naomi believes they do. She certainly talks to hers."

Jean Beede laughed. "So do I sometimes. I expect you'll end up doing that, too, Colonel." She looked at her watch. "William should be finishing with choir practice at the church very soon. You'll find him there, if you want to speak about the grass-cutting."

He took his leave of her and walked across the village green through golden sunlight and spreading shadow. She hadn't been able to tell him much more than he knew already but he stored it all away in his mind.

He passed the pond where the ducks were cruising about idly. The ducklings had grown to young adulthood and had lost their fluffy cuteness, soon they would be indistinguishable from the rest. The church clock was striking seven o'clock as he pushed open the old lych gate and went up the brick path that curved between the tombstones. A vase of pink roses stood on the still raw mound of earth over Lady Swynford's grave outside the west window, similar to the ones he remembered seeing on her dressing table. The sound of the organ playing and singing reached him as he approached the open door.

> The day Thou gavest, Lord, is ended,
> The darkness falls at Thy behest;
> To Thee our morning hymns ascended,
> Thy praise shall sanctify our rest.

It had been one of Laura's favourite hymns and he had chosen it for her funeral service. He stayed for a while just inside the porch, listening and reliving that agonising day.

> We thank Thee that Thy Church unsleeping,
> While earth rolls onward into light,
> Through all the world her watch is keeping,
> And rests not now by day or night.

The voices sang on – a mix of children with one or two adults. They weren't very good, except for one boy's voice that he could hear standing out with a high angelic purity. He waited quietly until the hymn was finished and, after a few moments, there was a loud clatter of young footsteps and a dozen or so boys and girls came racing out of the church. He stood aside as they passed by him, pushing and shoving, whooping and giggling in the way of all children released from constraint, and were followed presently by the adult choristers: a white-haired, shaky old man; a much younger one in thick-lensed spectacles; and a large woman wearing a print dress and cardigan. Another woman followed quickly on their heels, carrying a shabby leather music case, whom he recognised as the church organist, Miss Hartshorne. She consulted her watch as anxiously as the White Rabbit and hurried off down

*Old Soldiers Never Die*

the path without noticing him at all. When nobody else appeared, he went inside.

The Vicar was standing by the chancel steps, talking to a slight fair-haired boy who seemed upset and looked as though he were in tears. As the Colonel hesitated, they both turned his way.

"I'm sorry to interrupt . . ."

"Not at all, Colonel. Matthew is just going." The Vicar took his hand from the boy's shoulder. "Run along then, Matthew. You mustn't be late home. And try not to be too upset. Your mother may still change her mind."

The Colonel caught a glimpse of an ethereally pale and tear-stained face as the boy went past him, head bent.

The Vicar sighed. "Such a pity. That was our only decent chorister and his mother has said he can't come any more. Such a pity."

The angelic voice, the Colonel guessed. With features and hair to match. "What shame for you."

"It's even more of a shame for Matthew. His voice is quite exceptional and there was every chance of him getting into a choir school. Unfortunately, his mother won't hear of it. She's single parent, and doesn't want him to go away. I can understand it, of course, but it would have been a great opportunity for her son. He told me just now that she has forbidden him to sing in the choir any longer." He shook his head regretfully. "There was some kind of row, I gather . . . I'm afraid she thinks I'm a bad influence."

"I'm sorry. It must be hard to form a good choir."

"It is, indeed. In the main, the young aren't interested, of course; they'd much sooner be watching television or listening to pop music. They get pushed into it for a year or two by their parents and stop as soon as they can find a good excuse. Matthew was an exception. And it's just as hard to recruit good adult voices. I don't suppose *you* sing, do you, Colonel?"

"I'm afraid I wouldn't be much use to you," he said, guiltily ignoring the numerous amateur Gilbert and Sullivan productions that he had taken part in. "But I did come to offer you my services cutting the churchyard grass. I'd be glad to help if I can be of some use there."

"That's extremely good of you, Colonel. I'd be most greatful. Mr Townsend is in charge of our churchyard mowers rota. Perhaps you would give him a ring and you could arrange it between you?"

"I'll do that."

"Did you ever take a look at our famous tomb, by the way?"

"As a matter of fact, I haven't yet."

"Ah, well, now that you're here, you must."

The Swynford tomb was in a side chapel to the north and out of sight of the nave. Sir John Swynford and his wife Joan were carved in painted stone, lying side by side beneath a magnificent canopy with their hands held up palm to palm in pious prayer. Sir John wore armour, and Lady Swynford a ruff, gown and cloak. The rich crimson, black and gold colours of the monument had faded and flaked but were still easily discernible.

"It was erected in sixteen twelve," the Vicar said, holding his head on one side as he admired the tomb with the Colonel. "The paint is original. There was a proposal at the Parochial Church Council recently that the colours should be restored. I was not in favour of them being touched in any way myself and fortunately the idea was dropped."

"Fortunately," the Colonel agreed who had seen other well-meant restorations that had succeeded only in destroying the original.

"We have other treasures, too," the Vicar added, moving on. "This stained-glass window depicting sheaves of corn and grapes is medieval – bread and wine, you see. So is the squint, and we have a very fine brass to a fourteenth-century knight in front of the altar . . ."

They progressed gradually round the church and when they had finally reached and inspected the Norman font, the Colonel directed his gaze deliberately at the barrel vaulting above the nave.

"I hope the proceeds from the fête will be enough to preserve this fine roof of yours."

"It will stave off the worst trouble," the Vicar replied, craning his neck upwards, too. "We should be able to get all the leaks repaired and some timbers replaced so that it will be safe for a while. Of course, with a building of this antiquity it's an endless worry and expense. The annual fête doesn't begin to cover all the costs, but it certainly helps. I don't quite know what we'd do without it."

"I expect Miss Swynford will carry on the family tradition of it being held at the Manor."

"I certainly hope so. It wouldn't be quite the same anywhere else. The Manor is a great attraction."

"Would Miss Swynford be patron now, following the death of her mother?"

"Yes, indeed. Of course, she has no actual role to play just now where an incumbent has already been instituted, as in my case, but when I retire and the living becomes vacant then she will be required to present a new appointee to the Bishop."

"It all sounds rather medieval in this modern day and age."

The Vicar smiled. "Well, of course, there are other types of patronage. Sometimes it's a corporate patron, such as an Oxford or Cambridge College, or the Dean and Chapter of a cathedral. Or a bishop may have a number of livings in his gift. Or the patron is the Crown. It all seems to work very well. And I'm sure Ruth will make an excellent choice when it comes to the point. She'll have the guidance of the bishop, of course, and the PCC."

"She certainly strikes me as a very responsible person. And very charming. Her mother's violent death must have been a terrible shock to her."

"A dreadful thing . . . quite dreadful. A shock to us all. It could only have been an outsider, I'm convinced of that. A stranger who went to the fête with robbery in mind."

"And managed to get into the house and into Lady Swynford's bedroom where she surprised him?"

"Something like that must have happened."

"Did *you* notice anyone acting oddly, Vicar? Or anything that occurred to you later might have had some significance?"

He shook his head regretfully. "Nothing. The police asked me the same thing, but I couldn't remember noticing anything out of the ordinary. I was rather occupied, you see, going round all the stalls, I always try to do that, and talking to parishioners. In fact, I spoke to Lady Swynford myself, soon after she'd made her opening speech. That was the last time I remember seeing her."

"Was anything unusual about her? Her manner, or what she said?"

"No. We just talked about the weather – what a wonderful day it was, how lucky we were – and then she went on to speak to someone else – Mrs Cuthbertson it was, I think."

"You helped your wife get her wheelchair into the house, I believe, at around a quarter past four?"

"That's right. She had an idea that you might need a hand, someone to take over for a while. Typical of Jean, you know. She's extremely thoughtful for others. I got the wheelchair up over the steps at the side entrance for her, and then she said she'd be quite all right on her own. She insisted on it, so I left her there. She likes to be independent, you see. It's so important to her. I went and bought her a plant from Mrs Grimshaw's stall some time after that, I remember. I wanted to get her something. Jean loves her garden."

"Yes, she showed me round it when I called at the Vicarage earlier. It's beautiful."

"It was only a bare plot when we moved in, you know. She's wrought something of a miracle."

"Not quite alone, I understand. She told me how you'd built the special flower beds for her."

The Vicar's face softened. "There's so little within my power."

"You've done other things in the house, I gather. Switches, kitchen counters, ramps . . . She's fortunate in her husband."

He smiled. "No, Colonel, it's I who am fortunate in my wife."

The Major tweaked aside the living-room curtain and watched the Colonel go down the garden path, between Marjorie's regimented ranks of marigolds, and out of the front gate of Shangri-La.

What the devil had he been after? Coming here and asking questions. Snooping around. Supposing he was some kind of undercover agent? One of that secret army lot who pretended to be ordinary chaps and all the time they were digging up information, reporting back, *spying*. He clutched at the curtain like a drowning man. Had he given anything away? He couldn't remember what he'd said except that when the fellow had mentioned, ever so casually, that they'd bumped into each other as he was coming out of the Manor at the fête, he'd spun some story about having a gyppy tummy and having to find the downstairs thingummyjig. Well, that was true enough.

Ever since Malaya he'd been prone to a touch of the collywobbles, now and then. Damned inconvenient at times, too.

Thank God Marjorie was out shopping in Dorchester or she'd have known he was lying. Come to that, he wasn't too sure the Colonel hadn't as well. He'd given him a pretty hard look.

The Major mopped his brow. Had anyone else seen him, for God's sake? The thought made him sag at the knees and hold on to the curtain tighter. The old ticker was banging away in his chest and he felt as though he could hardly breathe. At this rate it wouldn't matter much, anyway – they'd be burying him in the churchyard, too, alongside Ursula. Well not *alongside*; they'd popped her with the Swynford lot in prime position, but in there somewhere. Might as well go and see that Inspector chappie straight away and give himself up. Face the music. Not that they ever had music in police stations, as far as he knew. He mopped his brow again and then took a slow, deep breath.

Wait a minute. Steady the guns! Rally the troops! Hold on to the horses! Take a good grip! Things weren't really so bad as he was making out. All he needed was a decent snort and he'd be right as rain. He strode purposefully towards the cocktail cabinet. Never mind about 'Drink to me only', Marjorie was miles away and not even she could hear it.

After a nip or two his courage returned, as though by magic. He could feel it seeping through him, warming his cockles – whatever they were – and stiffening the old sinews. He squared his shoulders, lifted his chin, braced himself, and felt like a new man. He was just polishing off the rest of his glassful when he heard Marjorie crashing the Escort's gears as she turned into the driveway and aimed at the garage. No need to panic, it would take her at least five minutes to get the damn thing in straight, to-ing and fro-ing and revving the engine like Stirling Moss . . .

## Old Soldiers Never Die

By the time his wife came into the living room the Major was sitting in his armchair, apparently deep in *The Times*.

Now, what was *he* doing here? Phillipa Rankin set down the bale of straw that she had been carrying across the stableyard and waited as the Colonel got out of his car and came towards her. Nice old car, she noted. Riley, wasn't it? Nobody made them like that any more. They all looked the same these days – Japanese, British, German – it didn't really matter. Her old Land Rover was twenty years old, but had scarcely given her a day's trouble. Not that she used it much now. Petrol was too expensive; the bike was cheaper to get around on.

"Good morning, Colonel." She shook the hand he offered, wiping her own down the side of her jodphurs first, as was her habit. "What can I do for you?"

"I wonder if you could give me some advice, Miss Rankin? I've got a four-year-old grandson who's just been on a visit. I hear you teach children to ride and I'm wondering how young they ought to start?"

She put one foot up on the straw bale. "The younger the better really. It's a bit like swimming, or skating or skiing, or just riding a bike. It's much easier to learn when you're young. Leave it too long and it's too late to be very good. But I wouldn't say there's a rush. I have some pupils around five or six years old and some a good bit older."

"When would you recommend him starting."

"Well, any time he wants to. Let him decide. And don't push him, whatever you do or you'll probably end up putting him off for life."

He nodded and looked around the stable yard. "I hope he'll be able to come here to you for a lesson or two. When he visits with his parents."

"By all means – if I'm still here."

"Oh? Might you be leaving?"

"Hope not. Rather depends on Ruth Swynford. I rent this place from the Manor. Have done for more than nearly thirty years."

"I see."

"Matter of fact, Lady Swynford had just raised my rent so the writing was on the wall, so to speak. Ruth tells me she's going to leave it at the old rate now. Jolly decent of her. I expect you've heard that on the village grapevine, anyway, Colonel."

"Would you have had to leave otherwise?"

"If Lady Swynford hadn't died, you mean? Probably. I couldn't see how I could go on for long at the new rate she was asking. It was nearly twice as much. I don't mind who knows it, I'm not too sorry she's gone – though, of course, I wouldn't have wanted her murdered."

"No, of course not," he murmured. "A dreadful thing to happen . . . and the police don't seem to be able to find out who did it, do they?"

"Too busy giving out speeding tickets, I expect. I had some inspector type here who thought he was the bee's knees. Kept asking me a lot of pointless questions about what I saw. I told him I didn't see *anything*. I was down in the paddock giving pony rides all afternoon."

"*All* afternoon? Without a break?"

"Except for when I went up to the house to the lavatory – gave the ponies a rest and popped up there. I was only gone about ten minutes, or so."

"To the house, you said?"

"Yes. There was a long queue at those Portaloo things and I knew where the downstairs cloakroom was from when I used to go up the Manor to give Ruth riding lessons, so I nipped in there. Didn't want to leave the animals unguarded too long. Some of those village kids are little beasts."

"What time would that have been?"

"Around four thirty, I suppose. I didn't notice. I know I was fairly desperate so it must have been quite late in the afternoon."

"Which door did you go in?"

"The side door. It was the nearest. I think the others were locked, anyway."

"Did you see anybody going in or out of the house, or inside when you were there?"

"Can't say I did. The cloakroom's only just along the passageway. Off the back hall."

"Yes, I know. My treasurer's counting house in Sir Alan's old study was right next to it. You didn't happen to glance in there? I believe Mrs Beede would have been in there, looking after things for me at that time?"

"No, I didn't. As I said, I was quick about it, Colonel. Didn't hang about. I was in and out in a tick." She folded her arms across her chest. "What's this all about, anyway? You're beginning to sound like that nosey policeman."

He said apologetically, "I'm sorry. I'm just rather curious. Nobody seems to have seen anything, and yet the murderer managed to get in and out. I wonder if they used the backstairs, just by the cloakroom."

"Hmm. I'd forgotten all about those . . . wouldn't have known they existed except that I opened the door to them by mistake once, years ago, looking for the cloakroom. Yes, maybe he did go up that way. They're much nearer than the front staircase and out of sight. In which case, he must have known the house pretty well."

"He?"

"Or she? Whichever it was."

"A woman would have needed to be fairly strong to smother someone. The victim would fight hard for life."

"I suppose so. I hadn't thought about that." She took her foot off the straw bale and bent to it pick it up again. "Well, just let me know about your grandson, Colonel, if he likes the idea."

She watched him with narrowed eyes as he got back into the Riley and drove off, and then carried the bale over to Petal's loose box. Now what had he *really* wanted?

# Thirteen

Ruth Swynford answered the phone to him.
"How nice to hear from you, Colonel. What can I do for you?"

He hesitated. "There's just one question I wanted to ask you – if you don't mind."

"Ask away."

"On the day of the fête, when you returned from the kitchen gardens and your meeting there, what time would that have been do you think?"

"I'm not exactly sure but I think it must have been about half past four. I do remember seeing you at the hoop-la when I got back to the lawn."

"What did you do then?"

"Well, I started off round some of the stalls again but the takings were tailing off and it wasn't worth doing a collection."

"Did you go into the house – into the study at all – while I was outside. Mrs Beede would have been in the study at that time, holding the fort."

"No. Definitely not. I didn't go indoors until quite a bit later and you were back there by then."

"I see . . . well, thank you, Miss Swynford."

"Please call me Ruth. Miss Swynford makes me feel old – which I'm getting."

He smiled to himself. "You've got a very long way to go."

"By the way," she added. "Inspector Squibb was round again. That padded envelope wasn't much help to them apparently, too many people handling it, including me, and there were no fingerprints at all on the brooch – not even my mother's. They found a microscopic piece of thread snagged on one of the diamond claws but it turned out to have come from the dress she was wearing that day. Do you know, I think the Inspector still believes I might have had something to do with it, now that they can't pin anything on Jacob. Murdered my own mother and posted the brooch back to myself. Can you believe it?"

She sounded on the verge of despair, he thought.

"Try not to let him worry you. They'll find out the real truth soon."

"I hope you're right. I'm beginning to be afraid they never will."

*I will*, he vowed to himself. "The postmark was Dorchester, wasn't it? Did they check at the post office, do you know, to see if anybody remembered it being weighed at a counter there?"

"I asked the Inspector that, but nobody did. The postage on it was far too much, so whoever it was obviously didn't risk getting it weighed, or anything."

"And the address was printed?"

"With an ordinary old biro, like millions of others."

"It was addressed to you personally?"

"That's right."

"How was it worded exactly?"

"Miss Ruth Swynford, The Manor, Frog End, Dorchester, Dorset."

"With the post code?"

"Yes, they'd put that too. Rather ironic, being so careful. Why on earth should they have worried?"

*Old Soldiers Never Die*

They finished the conversation and the Colonel put down his phone thoughtfully. He seemed to be going nowhere, except round in circles. It was certainly someone at Frog End who had sent back the diamond brooch. How many outsiders would have known the post code? Most people had enough trouble remembering their own. There was no evidence that the brooch had actually been stolen from Lady Swynford's bedroom. The clasp was faulty and it could have dropped off out of doors in the grounds – Laura had once lost a favourite brooch that way. Someone – anyone – might have picked it up and been tempted to keep it, not even knowing to whom it belonged, until they heard about the murder and panicked. And people with a guilty conscience about pinching things often sent them back anonymously – anything from library books to museum treasures. He could remember an instance when a piece of the regiment's mess silver had been returned like that. The brooch thief and the murderer were not necessarily one and the same. Or were they? God, this was no help to Ruth. He'd got to do better.

He got up and walked out into the garden, hoping it might somehow help him think. He inspected the alchemilla; he'd watered it religiously night and morning since planting and it seemed to have settled in well. The whole border was coming along and all his other new additions were looking happy. One or two were flowering away – Naomi's Hidcote lavender, for instance, which had grown considerably. He'd occasionally had a passing word for it, to give encouragement, amused at himself for doing so; but it was something to talk to, after all. He picked one of the flower heads and walked on, smelling it. The scent reminded him of the soap his mother had always used – Yardley's lavender.

Really, he'd learned almost nothing from his conversation with Major Cuthbertson who might, or might not, have been telling the truth about his emergency visit to the downstairs cloakroom; or from Phillipa Rankin, either, who certainly had the motive but barely the time – unless she had been away for much longer than she claimed, and that was perfectly possible. By her own admission, she had known about the hidden back staircase but if she were guilty and had used that route, surely she would have denied any knowledge of it? Considering the number of people who seemed to have used the cloakroom at some point during the afternoon – Miss Butler, the Major, Miss Rankin, Naomi, and himself, included, it was surprising none of them seemed to have bumped into any of the others. It had been like Piccadilly Circus.

Thursday appeared from nowhere and picked his way along the border, keeping his distance. He had sulked for several days after his banishment over Eric and still wore an air of injured pride. There hadn't been a word from Marcus for over a week now. Should he phone him, or shouldn't he? Was no news good or bad?

The Colonel and the cat reached the pond together and both stood gazing down into the now scum-free water. The frog spawn had disappeared long since, so with luck maybe there were tadpoles swimming around somewhere in the depths, or perhaps they were already frogs? He wasn't sure how long that took; it was too many years since his tadpole-keeping days. To have frogs at Frog End would be rather satisfactory. He bent down to peer closer but could see nothing living except water boatmen skimming across the surface. Perhaps he'd get some fish to liven things up – maybe even plant a water lily or two, then the frogs, if any ever appeared, could sit on the pads like Jeremy Fisher.

He went on staring into the pond for a while. Ruth hadn't been able to tell him whether Jean Beede had stayed in the study in his absence, or not, so he was no further forward on

## Old Soldiers Never Die

that track either. And surely it was complete fantasy to imagine that an arthritically crippled woman who spent most of her time in a wheelchair could have somehow got upstairs all by herself, have the strength to suffocate someone with a pillow and get back downstairs again, all in the space of half an hour. He had found her sitting calmly by the desk with the plant stall takings all correctly added up, hadn't he? Except that she could have simply copied his own figure from the note he'd made and never counted the money at all . . . and he had seen for himself that she had quite strong arms, hand-wheeling her chair along the border in her garden. *And* he remembered her telling him at that dinner party that she *could* walk, it was just simpler sometimes not to. But even supposing she was physically capable of carrying out the murder, what would her motive have been? Dislike of Lady Swynford because she was rude and unkind to her husband? As he himself had pointed out to Inspector Squibb, if people murdered for that sort of reason, there would be corpses wall to wall. Who else could be a suspect? The Vicar? But what possible motive could he have other than an understandable dislike for his patron? And he had left his wife at the door and gone off and bought that plant. Naomi, then? Murder in revenge for her sister's broken heart? He refused to believe it of her. *Unthinkable.* Which meant he was left with Jacob and his excellent motive, not to mention an unstable personality.

The Colonel tossed the bit of lavender into the water and straightened up. Perhaps he'd pay a call soon on Dr Harvey who might know something about disorders of that kind. And find out a bit more about rheumatoid arthritis. And tonight perhaps he'd ring Marcus. He strolled back to the cottage, taking another look along the border as he went. Thursday stayed sitting at the pond's edge, watching the lavender.

\* \* \*

London was like an oven; Waterloo Station a mass of sweaty, heaving, rush-hour humanity. As Ruth queued for a taxi she could feel the make-up she had so carefully applied in Dorset sliding rapidly off her face. Her linen suit was already a crumpled rag from the train. She fought her way to the taxi rank and the end of a long queue, and on the stop-start drive through heavy evening traffic she lowered the taxi window as wide as she could, past caring what any breeze would do to her hair. She had forgotten how swelteringly hot and noisy and crowded London could be. Ten months absence had turned her into a country mouse, gasping and gawping at it all.

At the restaurant Pierre greeted her as though she had never been away and ushered her to the usual corner table. She was early and Ralph was late and while she waited, smoking a cigarette and toying with a glass of wine, there was plenty of time to agonise all over again at her foolishness in coming at all.

But when he came in she instantly forgot her doubts. Watching him pause at the entrance, look for her and smile, was to go back in time; to feel exactly as she used to feel; to become that person again, hopelessly and helplessly in love with this tall, knee-quakingly good-looking man making his way towards her.

"Ruth . . . how wonderful to see you"

He took his usual place opposite her, back to the other tables in case anybody he knew saw him. Pierre brought menus and hovered discreetly. They chose the same sort of food they had always chosen and Ralph ordered the same sort of wine they had always drunk, and the same vodka and tonic with a twist for himself. He covered her hand with his.

"You're looking lovely. Different hair, isn't it?"

"I got it properly cut."

"I liked your country look too." He squeezed her hand. "You know, I never thought you'd come."

"Nor did I. But you seemed to think it was a good idea when we met in Dorset."

"*Extraordinary* coincidence, wasn't it? I still can't get over bumping into you like that. You actually living there, in that place."

"Fate at the fête, you might say."

He pressed her hand again. "You haven't lost your sense of humour then, Ruth, in spite of what's happened to you. I was so very sorry, when I heard about your mother. A dreadful thing! Simply appalling. I was going to call, but I wasn't sure whether you'd want me to."

"I wouldn't have minded." She had been so sure that he would, after how it had been between them that afternoon; had waited and waited for him to ring, actually. As it had turned out, in vain. It was she who had rung him.

"I read all about it in the newspapers, of course. Quite a sensation, unfortunately."

Splattered all over the front pages, in fact. And some of them had somehow dug up the story of Mama's past which of course had added to the fun: 'Baronet's Seven Veil Dancer Wife Found Suffocated'; 'Titled Temptress Topped'. She wondered if Ralph had seen those ones too, as well as *The Times*' and the *Daily Telegraph*'s more sedate versions. Poor Mama had tried so hard to keep that secret dark. She'd only found it out herself after Papa had died and she had come across an old nightclub poster rolled up at the back of a drawer in his desk.

"Yes, they made the most of it." She lit another cigarette.

"I don't remember you ever smoking, Ruth."

"I've taken it up again. It helps. So does the wine. Do you mind if I have another glass?"

"Of course." He snapped his fingers at a waiter. "Poor, Ruth, you must have been having a hell of a time. Have the police got anywhere with finding out who did it?"

"Afraid not."

"No suspects at all?"

"Except me."

"*You!*"

"Don't look quite so appalled, Ralph. Apparently, members of the family are always the most likely candidates, or that's what the Inspector kindly implied. And there's only me."

"I see . . . does he know anything about our meeting that day?"

"No. I didn't see any need to tell him." She watched the relief in his face and added, "I had to say I went down to the kitchen gardens because they were suspecting poor old Jacob and it helped to say I'd seen him there then, but I told them I'd gone to open the greenhouse windows. Perfectly plausible in that heat."

"Jacob? That gardener who saw us?"

"You don't need to worry about him. He hasn't said anything and he won't. He can barely string a complete sentence together and the police couldn't make any sense out of him."

"Frankly, Ruth, I'd just as soon it didn't become public knowledge."

"You and I?" She took a gulp of the wine that had been set before her. "You told me in Dorset, though, that you were definitely getting a divorce from your wife. Now that the children had both left home."

"I know. It's just that Helen hasn't been too well lately. She saw a consultant last week and it looks like she's going to have to go in for an op – one of those hysterectomy jobs. I can't really spring a divorce on her in the middle of all that. It wouldn't look very good."

Another gulp of wine. "No, of course not."

"As soon as she's back on her feet again, I'll do the deed, I promise. But there's no reason on earth why we can't go on seeing each, Ruth. When all this other business is cleared up."

"Other business?"

"Well, the police investigation. They'll be sniffing around, trying to find out everything they can, watching you . . ."

She set down her glass carefully. "As a matter of fact, Ralph, I was going to ask if you could help me there."

"Oh? How on earth could I?"

"Wasn't there someone high up that you knew at Scotland Yard – a commissioner, or something?" Ralph knew all kinds of people in all kinds of high places – cabinet ministers, judges, chairmen, generals, admirals. "I thought perhaps if you could speak to him he might be able to pull a few strings and get things moving down in Dorset. You see, it's terrible not knowing who murdered my mother, and pretty awful being a suspect too. I'm desperate for the case to be solved as quickly as possible."

He shook his head slowly and regretfully and, apparently, very sincerely. "I'm sorry Ruth, I don't really think I could involve him. He's not a *personal* friend, you know, and besides the police are very territorial. The Yard wouldn't involve themselves in something going on in Dorset without a very good reason."

He was making more excuses, she knew. And would go on making them. And on and on and on. The truth was that he was terrified of getting involved in a murder case; perhaps he even suspected her, too. And the truth was that he had no intention of divorcing Helen. Ever.

The waiter was setting the first dishes before them, *escar-*

*gots* for Ralph and *pâté de saumon* for her. Just like they usually had. She stubbed out her cigarette, tossed back her wine and groped for her bag on the bench seat beside her.

"I'm afraid I'm not hungry, Ralph. Thank you for the wine, though. It was nice to see you."

She stood up and went quickly towards the door. Pierre sprang to open it for her and she was out on the pavement, hailing a taxi that she could barely see for tears. Fool, fool, *fool*! Thrice times over she was a complete and utter and pathetic fool.

The London traffic was lighter now and the taxi driver fast. She was just in time to catch the next train home.

Dr Harvey's Renault was parked in his driveway. The Colonel glanced at his watch as he walked up to the front door. It was outside surgery hours so there was a good chance, for once, of finding the doctor at home and able to chat. It was a lovely old house, built of local stone: a big place for a single man, but then, as he knew, a large part of the ground floor had been converted into the surgery. He rang the brass bell and waited, wondering quite how he was going to broach a difficult subject. In his experience, though, difficult subjects were usually best tackled as frankly as possible and the doctor struck him as a man who would appreciate that rather than time-wasting flannel. Dr Harvey opened the door himself, and the Colonel hastened to explain.

"This isn't a surgery visit, Doctor. I know it's out of hours. But I wanted your professional opinion on another matter."

"Come in, then. You're lucky – you caught me before I go out on my afternoon rounds."

"I won't keep you long."

"Will ten minutes do it? That's all I've got, I'm afraid. Come into the study."

*Old Soldiers Never Die*

It was indisputably a man's room, not unlike the study at the Manor. Shelves of books, an untidy desk, plain walls and plain curtains, a few rather sombre pictures, one leather armchair for a visitor and not a frill or a flower in sight. The Colonel approved.

Dr Harvey waved at the armchair and went and sat behind his desk. "Right. Fire away."

"I'll come straight to the point. It's about Lady Swynford's murder."

"What exactly about it?"

"Miss Swynford seems to me to be in a particularly unpleasant situation. Quite apart from the shock and upset of her mother's murder, I gather the police have been treating her like a suspect."

"Have they indeed? It sounds the sort of thing Inspector Squibb would rather enjoy. Intimidating women. He tried that on with me, as a matter of fact. Wanted to read something into the fact that I took Ruth out to dinner once. I'm not quite sure what he had in mind, whether we were both supposed to have joined forces to do away with her mother, or whether I'd gone solo with one eye on the heiress. I cut him pretty short, whichever it was."

"Suffocation would be a rather unlikely choice for a doctor, I'd have thought, with easier alternatives to hand."

"I did point that out."

"I don't believe for one minute that Ruth had anything to do with her mother's death. I saw how shocked and upset she was for myself."

"Nor do I, Colonel. Not for even a second. And I share your concern for her. I wish to God the police would find the killer and clear the case up. If you've got any ideas, I'd be glad to hear them."

"Well, I've been wondering about Jacob the gardener at the

Manor. He did some work for me and he's certainly a pretty odd character. The police dug into his past and found out that he spent some time in a mental home, though they haven't been able to prove a thing against him. But the fact remains that Lady Swynford had given him notice some time before the fête and the man has a questionable mental history. I wondered what you thought about it?"

"He's not a patient of mine, Colonel, so I knew nothing about his medical history, but when Ruth told me about him I decided to do a bit of quiet investigation of my own. I found out the name of the place where Jacob was a patient and one of the psychiatrists there happened to be at medical school with me. Basically, Jacob's had problems since birth, wherever that took place. Nobody knows – he was left on a doorstep. He almost certainly suffered oxygen deprivation which caused all kinds of trouble: lack of co-ordination, speech difficulties, limited intelligence. Added to all that, he had a very traumatic time at a children's home: bullying, ill-treatment, and so on. It's a sad story. He turned his back on the world and grew his shell, and I can't say I blame him. He's like a tortoise: try to touch him and he instantly retreats. But he has no history whatever of violence. In my contact's opinion, and I hope to God he's right, it's extremely unlikely that he would harm anyone, let alone murder them."

The Colonel nodded. "Thank you. You've answered my first question."

"And your second?"

"Rheumatoid arthritis. What can you tell me about it?"

"It's a chronic disease causing pain and swelling in the joints, with resulting incapacity. That's it in a nutshell, unless you want me to go into gory details. There's no cure but it's treatable with anti-inflammatory drugs. There are periods of increased activity called 'flare ups', alternating with periods of relative remission. Does this still relate to Lady Swyndford's murder?"

"It could do."

"I'm not quite with you yet, but if this has anything at all to do with Jean Beede, I can't discuss her with you, Colonel. She's a patient of mine. Anyway, you're surely not suggesting that *she* could possibly have anything to do with the murder?"

"I'm not suggesting anything, I'm casting about for *any* possibility and she was left alone in the study at the Manor for at least half an hour, while I went outside. Speaking in general terms only, would someone in her situation be capable of getting upstairs and down again, unaided, and have the strength to suffocate someone? It sounds quite absurd, I know, but is it remotely possible?"

"This is turning into an interesting discussion, Colonel. My name should be Watson."

"You mentioned periods of remission."

"Which there can be, indeed. The painful swelling and weakness can fade and even disappear for a time."

"So it *could* be possible?"

"All things are *possible*, that's one thing I've learned about the human body. Given enough will-power and determination, it's capable of incredible feats. But, no, I don't think what you're suggesting is remotely likely. I'm afraid you'll have to look elsewhere, Holmes."

The Colonel smiled and rose to his feet. "Well, thank you, anyway."

Dr Harvey accompanied him out to the hall. "By the way, how are you sleeping now?"

"Oh, better. I chucked the rest of those pills away."

They shook hands and the Colonel walked away down the drive. On his way home over the green he passed by Lupin Cottage. Out of the corner of his eye, he caught sight of a slight movement at the bay window and a glimpse of a pale face behind the glass; Miss Butler was at her observation post.

He thought about her as he went by, tactfully pretending not to have noticed. Miss Butler had been one of those to make use of the downstairs cloakroom and had had the embarrassing task of telling Inspector Squibb about it. He himself had been responsible for that ordeal, but at the time he had only been answering a simple question. At some point that afternoon he had looked up and seen the back view of Miss Butler, going past the open study door. It had been later on, he was sure of it, after he had encountered her trying to guess the weight of the cake and after he had returned to the study. And, when he thought about it now, she had been going in the direction of the main staircase. The front door had been locked and so she must have come in through the side door, like everyone else, in which case she would have already passed the cloakroom *before* she reached the study. Perhaps she was simply trying to find it? But, surely Miss Butler would have been to a good number of fête committee meetings at the Manor and, long and tedious as they were, she should have had good reason to know where the downstairs cloakroom was.

The Colonel stopped and turned round. He went back to Lupin Cottage, opened the little gate and walked up the path to the yellow front door. He had to ring the bell twice before Miss Butler answered it. She stood there, staring at him wide-eyed, like some frightened animal, and he could think of no good excuse for calling. Before he could speak, she did, and in a faint, forlorn gasp.

"It's about the brooch, isn't it, Colonel? You've come about the brooch?"

# Fourteen

She faced him across the pin-neat and rather shabby little sitting-room of Lupin Cottage and he could see that she was trying to gather some shreds of dignity around her. Her chin had lifted and she was ramrod straight with her arms stiffly at her sides, as though on parade. *At ease*, he felt like saying.

"I know that it was a terrible thing, Colonel. A wicked, evil thing. And I must pay the price."

He was still in the dark. What terrible thing, precisely? Had she only stolen the brooch, or was there more?

He said quietly, "Perhaps you'd like to talk about it, Miss Butler? Just between the two of us."

She heaved a deep sigh and drooped suddenly. "Yes. Yes, I think I would. It's been such a burden on my conscience, you see . . . I have to speak to somebody. And I think perhaps that *you* will understand."

She was paying him a compliment, he realised, though he was not quite sure what he had done to deserve it.

"I'll certainly try."

"I stole the brooch, of course. You must have guessed that, or you wouldn't be here. It's almost a relief to confess."

"Go on. Tell me about it, Miss Butler."

"I have this unfortunate *trouble*, you see. So awkward to talk about." She was getting pinker in the face with every word. "Internal, you know."

A wide variety of female possibilities went through his mind, but no clue as to what this had to do with Lady Swynford's brooch. Miss Butler went on bravely, avoiding his eyes.

"I have to keep going to the bathroom . . . something pressing on something, apparently."

Light dawned. "I understand," he said quickly, to spare her blushes. "How very inconvenient for you."

"Oh, *very*. All the time. And it was getting worse. I could hardly get through meetings and things, and I couldn't sleep properly at night. I was getting so tired . . . When I went to see Dr Harvey he told me that an operation could cure it quite easily, but unless I go privately, which I could never afford, I'll have to wait such a long time before it can be done."

"So you stole Lady Swynford's brooch to pay for it?"

She bowed her head. "Exactly. When I saw it, it just came to me, all in a rush, that that was what I would do. She had so much, and she didn't deserve it. That's what I always thought about her, you see. I saw the brooch and before I could stop myself I'd taken it."

"*Where*, did you see it? On the ground, perhaps? On the Manor lawn?"

"In Lady Swynford's bedroom."

"You went up there?"

She nodded, her eyes still fixed on the floor.

"Miss Butler," he said slowly. "You told Inspector Squibb that you had gone into the house to use downstairs cloakroom."

"I did, Colonel. That was perfectly true. There was such a queue at the Portaloos outside and I find it so embarrassing waiting there in public with all the men, you know, and children giggling. And in any case, I really couldn't wait much longer. I slipped into the house by the side door and then, as I was there, I thought I'd just take a little look round. I knew the downstairs of the Manor, but I'd never been upstairs, you see. It seemed a perfect excuse. If I met anybody, I was going to say I was looking for the bathroom. Anyway, I thought that everybody was *outside*, including Lady Swynford."

"So you went upstairs? Then what?"

"Well, I opened a few doors – just to take a peep – and then I must have come to her room. I'd no idea at first that's what it was, of course, though I could see it was one of the main bedrooms."

"What exactly did you do, then?"

"I hadn't opened the door all the way, just a crack, but I could see a dressing table and the brooch on it. The sun was catching it, you see, and making it sparkle. I realised then that it was Lady Swynford's room, and that's when the idea came to me. To steal it."

"Go on."

"I darted in, picked it up and popped out again. I was in and out of the room in a second."

"Lady Swnford had been wearing that brooch earlier at the fête before she went upstairs to lie down. When you went into her bedroom she must have been there."

She jerked her head up and met his eyes. "I never saw her, Colonel. I swear it. I didn't stop to look at anything else in the room. I never even saw the bed. I just took the brooch and fled. I hid it in my handbag as soon as I got downstairs. It wasn't until afterwards, when I heard about the terrible thing that had happened to Lady Swynford that I realised that she must have been there all the time – perhaps asleep, perhaps already dead. I've no idea. Absolutely no idea at all. *I never saw her.*"

He had been studying her face closely while she spoke,

trying to decide whether she was telling him the truth. He had once been present at a court martial and watched the defendant stoutly protesting his innocence against overwhelming circumstantial evidence to the contrary. In the end the man had been proved innocent and acquitted. He had believed the man from the beginning. Miss Butler's story was just as incriminating, but the way she told it had also rung true. He thought back to that day at the Manor and remembered the layout of the room. Lady Swynford's bed had been behind the door, away from the direction it opened, and the dressing table directly in view. In her haste, Miss Butler, might well not have seen it. Then he thought of something else.

"The dog must have been there, on the bed, whether Lady Swynford was alive or dead. Surely he made some noise?"

"I didn't hear a thing, Colonel. But then Shoo-Shoo knows me quite well."

Useless animal, he thought. When it had mattered he'd been as much good as a hamster. Why the hell hadn't he barked or done something when his mistress was being murdered?

Miss Butler was twisting her hands together. "Later, I was so ashamed of what I had done. So *horrified*. And so frightened. I thought that if I confessed I had stolen the brooch I should be accused of murder. I didn't know what to do. In the end, I washed it and wiped it very carefully so there wouldn't be any fingerprints and I wore my gloves, just to be quite sure. Then I posted it back to Ruth. I don't suppose you'll believe me, Colonel, but I should have done that anyway. I could never have kept it. It was a moment of madness that I can't explain."

"Oh, I do believe you," he said gently. "And I believe the rest of your story, too."

She began to cry, putting her hands up to her face and

## Old Soldiers Never Die

sobbing. He led her to the sofa and made her sit down, sitting beside her and waiting quietly for her to regain control. After a while her sobs died away and she took the handkerchief he offered, and wiped her eyes.

"Of course, I'll have to tell the police now, I realise that, Colonel. It will mean a court case, prison . . . perhaps a *murder* charge. Thank heavens my dear father isn't alive. The disgrace would have killed him."

He followed her anguished look and encountered the admiral's ferocious and implacable gaze from the top of the bureau. Poor Miss Butler! Even with the admiral safely dead, her life would be in ruins. The quietly ordered existence, the respectable round, the safe little refuge she'd made for herself against a harsh world, would crumble about her. He made another decision.

"I see no reason for you to say anything at all to anyone at the moment, Miss Butler. Perhaps never. The brooch has been returned. You can shed no more light on Lady Swynford's death for the police. My advice to you is to keep silent at the present time. To wait and see. I suggest we both do that."

She turned her tear-mottled and astonished face to him and he saw the faint dawning of hope. "You really think so, Colonel? And you wouldn't say anything either?"

"Not unless it proves necessary. You have my word on that."

"Oh, *Colonel* . . ."

She started to cry again and he stayed with her for some time, holding her hand comfortingly in his.

He walked back to Pond Cottage later and got out the lawnmower to cut the grass. Then he trimmed edges and did some weeding. The garden was beginning to look quite reasonable, he thought. Apart from the happy herbaceous border, the honeysuckle was flourishing in its corner by the wall, the rambler rose was blooming away, the fruit trees were actually bearing fruit, and he was rather proud of his reclaimed pond. He was surveying it all with some satisfaction when the telephone rang and he went indoors to answer it. It was Marcus and he sounded more cheerful.

"I went for an interview this week, Dad, and they've offered me the job. I start next month."

"Wonderful news! Who is it with?"

"A firm in Norwich. They're quite new but I think they'll be growing fast. They make all different kinds of pasta, so it'll still be food. And, of course, it's what everyone's eating."

"Is it?"

"Oh yes. A lot of people have gone vegetarian and nobody eats as much meat. Cholesterol, and all that. Pasta's the 'in' healthy thing."

"Sounds promising, Marcus. Susan must be pleased. And you won't be so far from her parents."

"I haven't told her yet, actually."

"She's still in Essex?"

"As far as I know. We haven't spoken for a while."

"I think you should ring her, Marcus."

"I'm not sure I want her back, Dad. After the way she behaved."

"She was just upset and worried. That was very natural. Why not drive over and see her? Tell her about the new job, and talk it all over together?"

"I'll think about it."

When Marcus had rung off he poured himself a stiff whisky and sat down in the wing-back chair. He'd said the right thing about Susan, whether or not it would do any good. And it was excellent news about the job. Pasta had always been spaghetti, as far as he was concerned, but he had lately noticed other kinds at the supermarket in many shapes and different colours. Everything about the way people cooked and ate seemed to have changed so much. Wheeling his trolley up and down the aisles had been a revelation to him. There was a staggering variety to choose from and so many things he had never even heard of: sun-dried tomatoes, pesto sauce, walnut oil, balsamic vinegar and umpteen sorts of fancy mustards ranked alongside the only one he'd ever used – plain, good old-fashioned Colman's English. Even the pet food shelves offered a long menu for cats: salmon supreme, gourmet chicken, seafood platter, chopped beef in light gravy – and Thursday had the unpredictable tastes of a difficult and demanding old dowager.

He hoped to God he'd done the right thing with Miss Butler, as well. The plain fact was that he and she were both withholding evidence in a murder case. Perverting the course of justice, wasn't that the official phrase used? It had an unpleasant ring to it so, he'd better be right about her telling the truth, the whole truth and nothing but the truth.

He'd been thinking about that while he was gardening. And thinking about everything else, too. Going over it all in his mind, trying to find some kind of clue. To fit the pieces of the puzzle together.

He sat for a time, thinking and sipping at his whisky. For once he didn't notice the silence so much, or if he did, it didn't seem to bother him. After a while, though, he got up to put on one his records. When he had sat down again he leant back in the chair, drumming his fingers lightly on the arm.

> I stole the prince and I brought him here
> And left him gaily prattling
> With a highly respectable gondolier,
> Who promised the Royal babe to rear . . .

Think. Go over what Naomi had recounted. What Ruth had said. What Major Cuthbertson, Phillipa Rankin, Mrs Beede, the Vicar, Dr Harvey and Miss Butler had all told him.

> Time sped, and when at the end of a year
>     I sought that infant cherished,
> That highly respectable gondolier
> Was lying a corpse on his humble bier –
> I dropped a Grand Inquisitor's tear –
>     That gondolier had perished.
>
> A taste for drink combined with gout,
>     Had doubled him up for ever.
> Of that there is no manner of doubt –
> No probable, possible shadow of doubt –
>     No possible doubt whatever.

But he was full of doubts. Perhaps it *had* been been a complete stranger, someone who had intended robbery and turned to violence when Lady Swynford surprised him in the act. Except that most sensible thieves wouldn't choose a time in broad daylight when the place was crawling with people. Nor stop to rearrange their victim so carefully. So, go over it all again. Try another tack. Think of something someone had said or done that didn't add up. Maybe that would be the clue he needed to set him off on the right trail. Start again with Naomi standing in the garden, talking to him about the fête, and progress on from there. Go through everything the others had told him, however trivial it might seem. One tiny piece of the puzzle might make all the rest fit. *Think harder.*

And then he remembered one thing that didn't seem to make much sense. He considered it carefully for a while: looked at the implication, the possibilities. If for some curious reason it told him *who*, it still didn't tell him *why*. Or even *how* exactly. How had it been so easy? Then something else occurred to him, too.

He set his drink down and went to the telephone and dialled a local number. Mr Townsend answered and accepted his offer to be put on the churchyard grass-mowing rota with alacrity.

"Awfully good of you, Colonel. I'll put you down for the fourth week of every month, if that suits. By the way, my wife hopes you liked the dried flower arrangement she did."

"I'm delighted with it." He must remember to place it out prominently if either of the Townsends ever called. "As a matter of fact, I was rather curious to know who picked one of the other prizes."

"Oh, which one?"

He asked his question and Mr Townsend remembered at once. The Colonel put the receiver down thoughtfully. He had the answer he had expected, but there were puzzle pieces missing. *Why?* Unless, of course, it had something to do with what Ruth had told him. If it did, then he suddenly began to see what might have happened.

At first he thought that the church was empty. Without lights and on an overcast evening it was quite dark inside and the Colonel stood for a while, thinking himself to be alone, until he saw someone kneeling in a front pew. He waited quietly and, after a few moments, the figure rose slowly and turned towards him.

"I knew you were there, Colonel. And I know why. I can see it in your face. I know you have been trying to find out the truth."

"I'm right then?"

"Oh yes. But I don't know how you guessed. I thought I had been so very careful."

"I still don't know the reason, if that's any comfort."

"The only comfort I can find is in prayer, which is what I was doing just now: praying to God to grant me His forgiveness for my sin, and to tell me what I should do."

"And what did God answer?"

"That I must confess it. You seem to be on hand to receive my confession, Colonel. Would you mind?"

"Please go on, Vicar."

"I killed Lady Swynford because she found out about something that happened in my past, long ago, and she was going to have me removed from Frog End because of it."

"Could she have done that?"

"Not herself. A patron can't sack a priest, but proceedings may be brought against him for what is called a breakdown of pastoral relationships."

"Meaning what exactly?"

"Usually a scandal. Adultery with parishioners, for instance."

"Hardly applicable to you, Vicar."

"There are other forms of sexual impropriety, Colonel. Even less well received. Lady Swynford had found out about a court course I was involved in many years ago, before I ever joined the Church."

"What case?"

"I was accused of having an improper relationship with a ten-year-old boy – a pupil of my teaching days. Nothing was ever proved against me and the case was dismissed. I lost my job, as well as my reputation, but I managed to put it behind me and it belonged to the past, until Lady Swynford came up to me at the fête. She took a piece torn from an old newspaper from her handbag and showed it to me. It was a report on the case; there was even a photograph of me – easily recognizable. Except for my grey hairs I haven't changed that much. She just said, 'This is you, Vicar, isn't it? I'll be sending it to the Bishop and I'll make quite sure you're removed from Frog End.' "

"But that court case was long ago and there has been no suggestion of any similar complaints against you here."

"Unfortunately, there has. The Bishop recently received a letter from Matthew's mother – you remember that boy here that evening at choir practice? She claimed that I had undue influence on the boy, and implied a good deal more. It was a very unpleasant letter."

"Was any of it true?"

"I certainly did my best to encourage Matthew towards trying for the choir school. That was perfectly true. But as to any impropriety, I swear it's not so. I felt an affection and deep concern for him, but that's all. I had already explained that to the Bishop and I hoped he believed me. I doubt he would have continued to believe me after Lady Swynford had finished. But whether he did or not, she would have made quite certain that the whole village knew about it. My life would have been made miserable. My position as parish priest untenable."

"The case was dismissed, though."

"Would that have made any difference? People would still have wondered if I was guilty. You can imagine the disgust. The whispers. The finger-pointing. The sniggers. People will forgive and condone all sorts of misconduct but not that particular kind so easily. And once the story reached Matthew's mother's ears I would have had no chance of *anyone* believing me innocent. The press would probably have got hold of it before long . . . well, you can picture it all, Colonel."

He could, very vividly. "Did Sir Alan know – about the court case."

"Yes. I told him at the outset. He promised that it would

remain confidential between the two of us. The Bishop was never informed. I think I once said to you, Colonel, that Sir Alan gave me my chance."

"I remember."

The Vicar gripped the pew end, leaning on it for support. "What I did wasn't for myself, though, Colonel. It was for Jean. But she knew nothing about the murder. Nothing whatever. She is wholly innocent."

"Did she know about that case?"

"No, I never told her. It happened long before we met. I was always afraid that I might lose her."

"I think you did her an injustice."

"It was before I came to understand the sort of woman she is – far better and stronger and braver than I could ever be."

"Then why commit murder? She would have stood by you whatever happened."

"Jean is everything to me, Colonel. I would do almost anything to see that she doesn't suffer more than she all ready does. Can you understand that?"

"Oh, yes," he said quietly. "I can understand."

"I wanted her to be able to stay in the Vicarage, to have her garden to enjoy, and the benefit of all the things that make life so much easier for her. She's happy there and we could have stayed for years, until I retired. I didn't see why she should be uprooted and her life wrecked by a vindictive, spiteful woman."

"So you decided to kill Lady Swynford."

"I decided it when she had put the news cutting back in her handbag and walked away from me. And I knew I had to do it quickly. I couldn't imagine how, until Ruth came up when I was talking to Mrs Cuthbertson and said her mother had gone up to her room to rest. That was my opportunity, of course. I was worried about the dog, though."

"So you took chocolates to distract it?"

"How did you know?"

"I found out from Mr Townsend that you'd chosen the chocolates as a prize at the hoop-la. Chocolates give your wife migraine – she told me so – and it made no sense that you'd picked something she couldn't possibly enjoy. But the dog loves them."

"I'd seen Lady Swynford feeding them to the him many times. I took them out of the box and put them ready in my pocket and when I had helped Jean indoors with the chair, I slipped up the back staircase as soon as she was out of sight.

"You knew where it was?"

"When I visited Sir Alan during his illness I often went up and down that way because Lady Swynford never liked me using the front staircase. I went straight to the bedroom and when the dog jumped off the bed I emptied them all on to the carpet for him. Lady Swynford had her eyes shut and she didn't even hear me. I was going to strangle her with her scarf, if I could, but then I thought it would be easier and quieter with the pillow. It didn't take very long . . . I was surprised about that, though she did struggle a lot. Afterwards I did the best I could to make her look as though she was just asleep. I thought the longer it was before anyone realised she was dead, the better for me. Tell me, Colonel, did you guess because of the chocolates?"

"Because of the potentilla."

"I don't quite see –"

"You bought a bright red one, 'Gibson's Scarlet', from the plant stall for your wife, even though she doesn't like potentillas and she hates red flowers. That's what first made me wonder. She told me you must have forgotten, but I think you care far too much about her to forget something like that, any more than you would have chosen chocolates as a prize. It puzzled me until I remembered another thing Naomi Grimshaw told me that she had run out of newspaper wrapping for your plant but you found more under the stall table. It was the paper you took from Lady Swynford's bedroom, wasn't it? You couldn't leave it there with the piece torn out because it would have led straight to you, and you couldn't put it in your pocket or carry it around without people noticing because it was several large sheets, and you daren't throw it in a litter bin in case the police discovered it later. So you bought a plant – *any* plant – the first one you could get your hands on, and you used the newspaper as wrapping. That way, nobody would notice at all. And you could take it home and destroy it."

"It was on the dressing table. I saw it when I took the torn-out piece from her handbag. I used paper tissues when I was touching things, you know, so as not to leave any prints. I was so careful about everything. So very careful." The Vicar gave a deep sigh. "I don't understand how she came across that newspaper from so long ago. Twenty years or more. How was it possible?"

"I can tell you exactly how she did. Ruth Swynford bought a plant from the stall before the fête opened and Naomi wrapped it in one of the old newspapers her late sister had always hoarded. It just happened to carry the report on your court case. She just happened to leave the plant in the study and I gave it to Lady Swynford because it needed watering. When she unwrapped it before putting it in the sink she just *happened* to catch sight of your photograph and name. She took it up to her bedroom to read properly because her spectacles were there – I remember noticing them on her dressing table. Then she tore out the piece and put it in her handbag, ready to show you. It was all chance, Vicar: a chain of events."

"What a part that can play in our lives. I didn't take the diamond brooch, by the way."

## Old Soldiers Never Die

"I know you didn't."

"I keep wondering who did."

"Perhaps we may never know."

"So . . . now that you've heard my confession, Colonel. What are you going to do?"

"Inform the police."

"Before you do that, there's a favour I should like to ask you."

"A favour?"

"I sometimes go swimming at Lulworth Cove very early in the morning, before anyone else is around. It's a kind of therapy for me."

"Yes, I remember your wife telling me."

"Sometimes, when things have been very trying I've been tempted to simply go on and on swimming out to sea until it was too late to get back . . . to reach God that way. Not to have to struggle any more, simply to let go. If I were to do so tomorrow, would you agree to say nothing to the police? To spare Jean? The Bible says he that smiteth a man, so that he die, shall be surely put to death. Eye for eye, tooth for tooth, hand for hand, foot for foot. Would you be prepared to keep silent for her sake if that price was paid?"

"I might, if it weren't for Ruth Swynford. The police suspect her. And she needs to know the truth about what happened to her mother."

"Yes, of course, I hadn't thought of that. How selfish of me."

"I wouldn't say you were a selfish man, Vicar. Rather the reverse."

He smiled a desolate smile. "Thank you, Colonel. But if I wrote a full confession beforehand and left it to be found, would you then agree not to go to the police immediately? I could say I had done it in a moment of anger, but justice would be done and Jean would be spared the court case. Eye for eye, tooth for tooth."

The Colonel hesitated. "Your wife, Jean, if she could choose, she wouldn't want it that way."

"But it would still be best for her. She'll be without me, whatever happens. This way would be easier. People would be kinder."

"What would she do?"

"She has a widowed sister. We talked once about what she'd do if anything happened to me . . . she said that her sister would take her in. They've always been close."

"You're asking a great deal of me."

"I know. I wouldn't ask it of someone else. But I know *you* will understand. And I beg you most humbly."

The church clock began to strike the hour, each note loud in the silence. Before the last had died away, the Colonel had made up his mind.

# Fifteen

"Have you decided what you're going to do, Ruth?"
"Only to do nothing much – for the moment."
"You'll stay in Frog End."
It was more a statement than a question and she was rather amused. "Is that medical advice, Tom?"
"It's good commonsense. You belong here. You're among friends and people you know. That counts for a lot."
She moved over to the French windows and looked out onto the garden. Jacob was working on the border and she watched him bending jerkily up and down to the plants, like a puppet on strings. Shoo-Shoo, was lying on the lawn, not far away. Mama would have been horrified by his unclipped state, but she thought he looked much better.
"As a matter of fact, I've had this idea for a while to start up a sort of garden centre here. Raising my own plants for sale, and having the gardens open for people to look round and get ideas. Perhaps some talks on different subjects, that sort of thing. Naomi said she'd give me a hand. It probably wouldn't work, but it's a thought."
"It's more than a thought. It's a future. And I'll be around."
She said, still amused. "That's the title of a song."
"Then somebody else felt just the same."
When Tom had gone she went out to give a hand with the

border. The heavy rain last night had flattened a lot of the plants and weeds seem to have sprung up all over the place. It was enough, for the moment, to think about the present and the work that needed to be done.

"You know, just for a while, Roger, I wondered if *you* might have done it."

The Major swivelled his head sideways. "*Me*? Good God, Marjorie! Whatever gave you that idea?"

Mrs Cuthbertson swung the Escort giddily round a sharp bend. "Well, I thought she might have made fun of you. You know, really upset you, so you'd gone and lost your head completely. But then I said to myself, no, he'd never be capable of it. Not Roger."

From her tone it dawned on him that this was not a compliment.

"Matter of fact, old girl, I thought the same thing about you, for a bit."

She stared at him in astonishment. "Why on earth should *I* have wanted to murder Ursula Swynford?"

"Well . . . jealousy. Me and her. And all that – *for God's sake watch the road, Marjorie!*"

She was actually laughing as she wrenched at the wheel. The front wing on his side clipped the hedge and torn leaves and broken branches showered the bonnet.

"Good heavens, Roger, jealous over *you!*"

"I can't see why that's so funny."

She was still smiling. "No, I suppose you can't. Anyway, there was never anything to be jealous about, was there?"

He didn't answer. How could she be so sure? Damn it, he wasn't over the hill yet. Not by a long chalk. And things had been getting pretty steamy with Ursula. She hadn't really meant what she'd said to him at the fête – he'd decided that long ago. He'd definitely misheard, what with that bloody band making such a damned racket.

His blood still ran cold, though, when he thought of how he *might* well have been suspected. What a damned fool he'd been blundering about the Manor. God knows how he hadn't been spotted, except by the Colonel on the way out, of course, but he'd been pretty quick on his feet with an explanation there. He'd only wanted to find Ursula, talk to her, and then when he finally *had* found her, lying up there on the bed, he'd realised she was dead. Jesus, that had been a hell of a shock! Of course, he'd thought she'd gone and had another stroke, and the only other thing he'd been able to think of at that precise moment was what Marjorie, not to mention the whole village, would say if he had to admit to being up there, in Ursula's bedroom. Not even he would have been able to think of a good one for that.

As for when he heard she'd been murdered . . . well, he didn't think he'd had a decent night's sleep ever since. Not till the Vicar had owned up. The *Vicar*! Damned poor show, really. Man of the cloth, and all that. Supposed to know better. Even the old girl had been surprised and she always thought she knew everything.

Well, she didn't know the half of it. Didn't understand him at all. There was plenty of life left in the old dog yet, and plenty of time for him to learn new tricks. Many a good tune was played on an old fiddle. Yes, by Jove, he rather liked the sound of *that*. And there were lots of good fish in the sea. Well, not so many in Frog End, perhaps, but maybe he could do a spot of casting around elsewhere.

He frowned. Dogs? Fiddles? Fish? Damn it, he was off again with those confounded silly sayings.

He clutched at the door handle as Marjorie swerved into a right turn. The Escort bounced along beside the village green like a kangaroo.

The Major sighed. Every dog was supposed to have its day. He wondered when he was going to have his.

Miss Butler had the U-boat captain's binoculars trained closely on the Cuthbertsons' car. Mrs Cuthbertson was driving – she would have known that by the way it was jolting along, even if she hadn't been able to see her clearly, crouched over the wheel. The Major must hate that. In her experience men never liked being driven by a woman; Father had never stopped grumbling about the WRN drivers. Still, the Major would soon be getting his licence back, though maybe that wouldn't be such a good thing when she thought about it.

She followed the Escort until it veered into the driveway of Shangri-La and then she did an exploratory sweep across the green, focussing on another car emerging from the Manor entrance. Interesting . . . she'd noticed Dr Harvey's grey Renault coming and going there a number of times lately and something told her that there might be a little romance brewing in the air. Now, *that* would be very satisfactory. Both so well suited and both so nice. Dear Dr Harvey who had managed to get her put ahead on the consultant's waiting list so that it would only be a matter of weeks now. And dear Ruth who was such a kind person. Always so civil and considerate, and look how she had let Miss Rankin go on paying a low rent and kept that poor, unfortunate young man on at the Manor. She tracked the Renault until it disappeared round the corner and then swung the glasses back across the green again. Like their original owner, about whom she had sometimes wondered, she came to an abrupt and predatory stop as she sighted a new quarry. Mrs Grimshaw was on her way round to the Colonel's cottage and she seemed to be carrying something that looked like a pot of jam. There was a

## Old Soldiers Never Die

good deal of to-ing and fro-ing there too, but, of course, no suggestion of any entanglement in that particular case. No one could ever think that – not with Naomi Grimshaw. And the Colonel had obviously been very much in love with his late wife, and was, in any case, a perfect gentleman. There were not many of those left these days. Such a handsome man! That tall, military figure. So distinguished-looking. So understanding. So *chivalrous* – that was another quality that sprang to mind and equally rarely found any longer. He had come to her rescue like a knight in shining armour. Miss Butler watched Naomi Grimshaw hammer on the front door of Pond Cottage and then barge inside.

She lowered the heavy binoculars. The Colonel had never breathed a word of their little secret and she trusted him completely never to do so, now that there was no need. Who would have thought the Vicar would have done such a terrible thing? He had seemed such a gentle sort of person. But then Lady Swynford had always treated him disgracefully, so perhaps it wasn't so surprising, after all. She'd felt she'd hated Lady Swynford herself at times, though not, of course, enough to *murder* her just rather wish her not alive, which wasn't *quite* the same thing. The Vicar must have been goaded beyond endurance . . . poor, sad man.

She swept the village green once more. Nothing much seemed to be happening so she hid the glasses away in the bureau – it wouldn't do for anyone to see them. Though, of course, as an admiral's daughter, it would be perfectly natural for her to own such a thing. Father was looking a little kinder this evening. Not quite so critical. Almost forgiving, though perhaps that was only her imagination.

The clock on the mantelpiece struck seven. Time for supper. Not sardines or poached eggs, for once. She was going to treat herself to a small lamb chop – lightly grilled, and with some new potatoes and frozen peas. It was an extravagance, of course, but she felt like celebrating. She had been given her life back again. She moved towards the kitchen, humming a little tune.

"Sad about poor old William," Naomi said. "Still, I suppose there are worse ways to go. People say drowning is quite pleasant, though I don't know how they could possibly know." She had plonked herself down on the sofa, dressed in a fuzzy white tracksuit that made her look like a polar bear. "Never suspected him for a moment, did you? Odd he went and did the deed then and there. I imagine Ursula said something nasty, as usual, and he just snapped. The worm turned in the end. Served her bloody well right, in my view. Treat people like dirt and in the end it'll come back at you with a vengeance. Ah, thank you, Hugh. Very welcome. Chivas, as usual?"

Having handed over her glass of whisky with a splash, no ice, the Colonel retreated to his wing-back chair.

"Cheers, Naomi."

"Bottoms up, and all the rest of it." She took an appreciative gulp. "Aaah . . . that's better. You know, when I heard he'd done it, I thought maybe Ursula had found out about William's guilty past and held that over him. Just the sort of bitchy thing she'd do."

"Guilty past?"

"I can tell you now because it doesn't matter much any longer, and I know you'll keep it to yourself anyway."

Why was it that everyone always trusted him implicitly not to repeat things, he wondered bemused. How could they be so damned sure?

Naomi carried on blithely. "There was a court case years ago – monkey business with a small boy, you know. He got

*Old Soldiers Never Die*

off, but Jessica and I always reckoned he was guilty. What are you staring at me like that for, Hugh?"

"Nothing. I was just thinking . . . how did you know about it?"

"We noticed it in one of the old newspapers when we were clearing the Hall out. There was a long report on the front page and a big photo of William – he looked just the same, except that he wasn't a clergyman then. It was the boy's word against his, and nothing was proved, so the case was dismissed. But it all sounded a bit odd, and we always thought he might be a bit like that. People can't help it, can they, but they mustn't mess around with kids. Poor old William! So devoted to Jean, so anxious to please everybody, so conscientious, *such* boring sermons."

"You never said anything to anybody? Not a word?"

"Don't look so amazed. Certainly not. I don't tell tales out of school, and nor did Jess. I'm all for juicy gossip, but not the sort that destroys people."

"You restore my faith in human nature, Naomi."

"I didn't know you'd lost it. Actually, I thought you might be hot on the scent yourself, with all your questions."

"Oh, not really."

"Pity. I wanted you to beat that Inspector Squabb at his own game. As it was he had it all dished up to him on a plate. Suicide note, complete with full confession. Body washed up."

"Squibb, not Squabb."

She waved the glass. "What's the difference? He's a nasty piece of work, by any name. Poor Jean, I felt badly for her with him crowing about the place like a cock on a dungheap. I think she might have suspected the truth all along, you know."

"Why do you think that?"

"Oh, just a hunch. She's nobody's fool."

"Do you know what she's going to do now?"

"Go and live with her widowed sister. Not a bad thing. They get on well and the sister lives in a bungalow. *And* there's a garden. She's got plenty of guts and she'll be all right. Speaking of gardens, yours is coming along pretty well, isn't it? I took a peek over the wall today. We'll make a gardener of you yet." Naomi tossed back the rest of her whisky in one go and stood up. "I must be off. Brought you some home-made jam, by the way. Stuck it on the hall table when I came in."

"Thank you. I'll enjoy it."

"See that you do."

At the front door she paused, considering him with her head tilted to one side. "You're looking much better, Hugh. A different man. I was quite worried about you when you first arrived, you know."

"Well you know the saying about old soldiers, Naomi."

"They never die?"

"They just fade away."

"Well, you won't be doing that for a long while."

She strode off down the pathway and he picked up the jar she had left on the side table. Rasberry Jam. He smiled. That was more like the old Naomi that he knew and liked so well.

As he went back to the sitting-room the phone rang and Marcus's voice sounded in his ear.

"I took your advice, Dad. Got in the car and drove to Essex to have it out with Susan. We talked it all over . . . she's back now, with Eric. I brought them home."

"Well done, Marcus. Well done."

He went out into the garden. The air was still, the evening light soft and golden, and a blackbird was singing from the top of one of the apple trees. Thursday appeared from nowhere and shadowed him at a casual distance as he carried out a tour of inspection. He gave a word or two of praise and encouragement here and there. There was no doubt that it was all coming along nicely – even Naomi had given her nod of approval. Alison would be quite surprised when she saw it next weekend.

As he reached the pond a sudden small movement caught his eye and, bending down, he saw a frog squatting at the edge. For a moment they eyed each other, motionless, and then the frog leapt forward and plopped into the water. Now, at last, he had his frog at Frog End.

He walked on down to the rough patch of grass at the end where the fruit trees grew. There'd been a bulb catalogue in the post that morning so perhaps later on he'd sit down and go through it and plan what he might order to plant for next spring. It would be nice to have a whole lot of daffodils and narcissi here, in drifts like Naomi's – he'd try just chucking them down like she did and planting them where they fell. He'd be able to see them from the kitchen window and watch them growing.

The blackbird was still trilling away loudly on his high branch, beak wide, and he stopped to watch it and listen for a while. Naomi had been right: he did feel better. He still had his uses, apparently. Life could still have some point to it. He strolled slowly back to the cottage, taking a last look along the border, the old cat following.